Soul

Thieves

Graeme K Parker

Copyright © 2023 Graeme K Parker

All rights reserved.

ISBN: 9798853280571

Dedication

I suppose this should be dedicated to those that helped me write it. Sadly, however, nobody assisted or encouraged me. My daughter did say it was "okay" after the first printing, so I guess the dedication goes to her.

Google was great for spellings, definitions, answering question about MS Word, and a little research. Thanks to Larry and Sergey for that.

Commas were added and removed by grammarly.com. As was capitalisation and the odd escaped apostrophe.

Cover artwork created using playgroundai.com

Forward

Death, the final frontier. Or is it?

That depends upon whom you ask. If you ask a religiously inclined person for their take on death, the consensus is likely to be that it is the start of the rest of your existence in some form of afterlife. Whether you terminate in purgatory is another matter entirely.

If you hear the replies from atheists, agnostics, and sceptics, then death is final.

Nobody truly knows, but this story pays heed to the first set of views. But perhaps, if the journey could be retraced, then the sceptics could be persuaded.

This story, a dream I once had, could answer this question once and for all.

Alvar in his Counting House

Life isn't simple, Alvar thought as he dangled the last remnants of a deathly soul from his blade and let them fall onto the cobbled study floor to disappear through the dusty cracks. If my subjects would just do as they were commanded, then there'd be no need for this torture, this humiliation, for this pleasure!

Alvar sat with contempt for his subjects and watched the soul depart swiftly with a smile growing wide upon his face. This experience was a pure pleasure for him.

His latest victim, that had just sunk into the cold stone, was merely an old traveller and his crime was simply to refuse to bow and show fealty when Alvar's cortege trundled past the boundary gate into the City. Noticing the traveller's apparent disdain for Alvar, his pomp, and the gaudy decoration of his carriage, he halted his carriage and stepped down onto the dry dusty earth.

"Beggar, do you not know who you impudently gaze upon? You should step aside and show some common courtesy to your King."

The old man, leaning on his tall knotted staff and who'd obviously seen many good years and too many recent dire ones, replied, "I see a man with a wealth of possessions, but you can't measure a man's wealth by the gold alone that he can carry."

Alvar started to listen and hear what else this man was going to say to condemn himself.

"Take the lepers living near the old salt mine, they

have respect, sympathy, and families who love and care for them. Is that not more riches than you can hold in your treasure chests?" the old man continued.

"That would appear to be a veiled insult, but I assume you are not from these parts. Perhaps you should be forgiven your stupidity, and…"

"There is no veil. What I tell you is honest, from my heart, and from the minds of others too. And who will forgive you for your stupidity?" the traveller interrupted.

It was quick. Alvar, impatient and intolerant, did not want to hear any more, and did not hesitate. The traveller's crumpled body lay across the dusty path, the last remnants of his soul being stoppered in a golden vial glistening and crackling in the outstretched gloved hand of the King.

"Take the body and burn it! I trust that your service is not in question. I don't want to hear rumours of my noble deeds spreading amongst my people, lest you wish a similar fate."

The footmen approached the body cautiously, for it may be lifeless, but death lingers in the remnants of the soul, and the fingers of death hold tight if you become entangled in their grasp. Alvar climbed into his carriage and pocketed the vial. This would provide his entertainment tonight.

Perhaps not a typical day for those that Alvar received no respect from, but these actions were still all too frequent in recent months. Mysterious disappearances, murders such as this in broad daylight, and yet he still had command of his armies and his realm.

Alvar in his Counting House

Alvar sat and leaned back with his boots placed firmly on the desk in front of him, tilting his chair and balancing onto its rear legs. He played with the dagger in his hands, spinning it into the air and catching it on its return into his palm. He glanced around his study at the myriad of vials, canisters, and other containers. Each one held something that could be used to gain power from or over mortals. Some containers held matter that was not from the living world, but these were well hidden from visitors' eyes.

He had recently emptied the contents of such a bottle onto his desk. The squirming mass had twisted and writhed before departing into the floor under the encouragement of Alvar's blade. These had been the remnants of the beggar's soul captured earlier that day.

The King had not the ability to perform any major magic with these lost ones, but did have the necessary knowledge on how to use them as weapons. And their use, when employed privately, would leave no physical sign of attack, simply a dead body.

The preparation of his weapon was a dangerous procedure, similar to loading a crossbow with the bolt facing you, one slip, and it would be your life lost. The soul-taking canisters needed to be armed like the bow. Each one needed to be part-filled with a small piece of a long-lost soul. A soul many years absent from its body, and anxious to advance to its final peaceful resting place, or to attempt to cling to life in desperation. The soul would be spilt into many parts, each acting as a catalyst for the seizure of another. Souls attract souls. The bottles were charged with these torn and divided souls, and breakout from their prison was dissuaded by the metal collar around the bottle's neck. Thus, Alvar's arsenal was constructed.

The King slid his feet from his desk and the chair fell forward catapulting him to a standing position. He thrust the knife's point firmly into the oak desktop where it joined with many other gouges, vacated his study and entered the atrium, pulling the study door closed securely.

It seemed to be an uphill task, trying to persuade his loyal subjects that loyalty was really the best for them. But allegiance was not something he was assured of from any of his countrymen. On the contrary, when he assumed power, albeit via a quick and painless battle, for him, he made no friends. The deposed King was well respected, and loved even, but the new one, well, he wasn't going to be on many people's guest list come feast time.

He knew that the senior lords of the great houses in his country would condemn his actions at every opportunity, but never ever to his face. That would be the last thing they ever did, as the array of trophies upon his walls would testify. Decorating his walls were swords and crests from several fallen houses, their masters being disposed of after Alvar had learned of their dissatisfaction with him as ruler.

He had managed to maintain loose but cordial relations with the surrounding towns and villages, of

Alvar in his Counting House

which there were a few dozen within a day's ride by horse or carriage. The main purpose was to provide taxes for the King. Taxes that all were reluctant to have levied upon them, for in return they received very little of real value. This revenue was used by Alvar to maintain his chosen lifestyle and his armies. He made no secret of his powerful military that was funded in this way, for he used this as the primary reason for the payments, to defend against an outside aggressor. To defend himself.

Unfortunately, there were seldom acts of war undertaken on any localities, so Alvar's excuse of armies for defence was without standing. Opportunely though, his accumulated wealth, essentially stolen from his citizens, was easily sufficient to employ the services of mercenaries, and private militia, who could put on a convincing disguise and assault his own populace.

The local settlements would be squeezed for their monies, but, when times were hard and a harvest was poor or blighted by disease, there was no help forthcoming from their King.

And so life went on in this endless struggle.

For Alvar, this situation was not acceptable, change was needed. The obedience of his citizens was an obligation that they must provide. He cried out to be accepted in the same way as his predecessor, to be the kingdom's true leader. But he had not the knowledge and sense of duty as did King Godwyn before him. Alvar was purely a schoolyard bully.

A decision was made, and he sent word for a

gathering of his generals and treasurers.

In the courtyard immediately surrounding the main entrance hall to the castle, a steady stream of decorated and immaculately attired army elders was arriving, descending from their mounts and carriages, each general being accompanied by two or three assistants. All were greeted by the King himself and escorted through the gate and into the lavish banqueting hall.

Interspersed within the generals' appearance, a small company of dark-attired bankers slipped from their coach and entered Alvar's residence. They were familiar with such appointments, since presenting collected taxes was a frequent event, but were also cordially greeted and invited to join with the expanding collection of guests.

The King's hospitality to his favoured guests was not in question. Of course, there was always a reason for a social gathering at the castle, and this occasion was not to be an exception. It was a peculiar spectacle to observe the two distinct groups of people undertaking any action necessary so as not to mingle. The generals were conversing in one blaring company, gulping fine wines by the flagon, whilst the more timorous bankers were more or less huddled over in a dim corner of the hall, hiding from all others.

The assembly was complete. The generals and bankers from Abeline were all present as requested, so now to business.

The main doors burst open and Alvar strutted in with as much pageantry as he could muster. As the doors gently closed behind him, and the attention of his guests was drawn to himself, he opened his arms wide in a welcoming gesture and forced an uncomfortable smile onto his face.

"My friends." This would've been far more convincing from the lips of King Godwyn, but Alvar was endeavouring to be gracious and appreciative of their presence.

"We have an evening of exceptional cuisine and select wines, some business details to discuss of course, and entertainment to soothe and jollify your hearts."

He pointed to the banqueting table lavishly adorned with a wide variety of cooked meats, game and fruit. Together with flagons of ale, decanted wines, and classy candelabras, the impressive scene that they beheld was nothing short of magnificent, and plenty to feed a large household for a year.

The King's minstrels began to play selected bright melodies, as Alvar directed his guest to take their places for the feast. Strictly speaking, the minstrels were in the employ of the queen, Ophilya, and were more at ease in her company than her husband's. Ophilya knew that skilled musicians could perform compositions that would have a soothing effect on the consciousness and open the listeners' minds to suggestive instructions. Not for any lurid effects, but primarily to take advantage of her opponents during simple games of cards.

The general's acceptance of the King's hospitality did not need any encouragement and they were immediately at ease with the situation, quaffing the King's mead and filling their mouths with juicy meats and game. The bankers and accountants had become somewhat more relaxed and too were feasting contentedly.

Alvar was now steering the conversation topics in the direction of his primary goal, to create strategies to subdue any upcoming rebellion. He had had word from people in the West, who appeared to be paying the highest taxes, that their discontented condition was coming to a head. Demonstrations had taken place, and rebellious leaders were being heralded.

"You know, of course, that the behaviour of my citizens will affect us all." He looked around the table as the feasting began to subside in all quarters.

"Insurgency will inevitably lead to fewer monies gathered from taxation, which has the consequence of not being able to afford such large unused armies." He directed this explicitly at the generals on his right. "And less money to manage requires fewer bankers." A stable life and future was the bank workers' greatest hope in life, so the implication that there would be redundancies quickly took the grins from their greasy faces.

"And your proposal is? I assume that's why we're here," asked a large, moustached gentleman on the general's side of the table.

"Well, I believe it is quite straightforward, simple even." Alvar was now standing and addressing the gathering.

"Divert some funds into the hands of your favourite mercenaries. I'm sure you can find some of these butchers that you can rely upon, and make use of their services secretly. Request that they pay a visit to the troubled regions, and, as a bonus, terminate the dissenters and especially their leaders."

Alvar took another bite from the greasy pheasant leg in his hand and continued. "Killing, so to speak, two birds with one stone. The poor citizens will relent and agree to my taxation, and the insurgency will be crippled without any direction."

He raised his eyebrows in anticipation of an outburst of questioning, but none was forthcoming.

"So be it!"

Lost

Eva threw her books casually into her soft leather satchel and strapped the cover closed. She slung the heavy bag over her shoulder and bent down to pick her soft canvas bag from the floor. All of her fellow students were already leaving the study room and making their way to the outer courtyard, stopping off via the secluded dark changing rooms to replace their normal wear with freshly washed outdoor clothing fit for a more energetic lesson.

She didn't mind most of the theory lessons, and welcomed the practical ones. But when it came to compulsory outdoor games, she had her favourites, and that afternoon did not include any of them.

Her formal education, like that of many of the well-off families' children, continued well past the age where lesser families would be sending their offspring to work. If she continued beyond what was the norm for her status, she'd be well into her twenties before pursuing a career or, god forbid, a family of her own.

Eva reached the changing rooms as the last of the students were leaving, several of them looking behind over their shoulders at her as she made her way to her normal seat. Draped over the rusty nail that sufficed as a clothes peg hanger was a dead mouse. It was not fresh and rigor had long since set firm in the small brown lifeless body. This was not the first time a gift had been left for her. In fact, it was becoming the norm but Eva ignored the creature and simply moved to one of the remaining pegs.

Of course, she had heard rumours but did not want to believe everything she had heard. What her few friends had recounted was not something that she took seriously during a conversation, but within her, she knew that there must be some truth. Rumours about her birth. But how many people believed in these?

She sat heavily upon the bench and paused for a moment before bending forward and removing her shoes, trousers, and then shirt. She pulled her one-piece white dress from her bag and slipped it over her head, fastening a thick cord around her waist for a belt. A small ribbon secured her long tousled hair away from her smooth cheeks and out of her eyes.

She ventured outside into the bright Summer sunshine and lined up with her fellow classmates in a row, ready to be selected for the two teams. Today was the last sports day of the year and so it would be two teams competing in all of the sports. All the ones that Eva disliked the most. Her long list was headed by kickball, then handball, and indeed anything that included the boy's favourite sporting item. Where was the inclusion of sports that she particularly excelled in; throwing sports, fighting sports, fencing?

Taking her place she waited to be called, and called last if history was to be relied upon.

True to her estimation, she was selected even after the short but large girl. "Eva. Red Team!"

As she strolled unwillingly towards her captain it was

quite obvious that she had no intention of playing the good student and giving this exercise everything, or indeed anything.

"You're in goal," her captain said and pointed back towards the netted opening behind her.

"Really?" she inquired. "That's a novel decision!" Whilst the game held no interest, the players on her team were the best and it was very likely that she would not be engaged in defending her net for the duration of the match. Time for some idle thoughts.

And her thoughts, after the start bell was rung, soon veered towards the primary questions that sat rigid in her mind so very often. Why am I without a family?

This was a question whose answer had eluded her ever since she realised that family life normally meant the presence of parents and perhaps siblings. For the last six years of her schooling, she had looked on at other children's parents collecting them at the end of lesson time.

When her guardian arrived, Eva perceived the woman as a lonely but always happy lady, and the hugs she received without fail every day made her both happy and sad inside. Inward tears as to why her dad would never embrace her, and inward tears when she was hugged tightly by the person she loved the most in her life.

But the hugs would surely lessen as Eva turned into a woman. These were the times that she was most concerned about. Life had a repetitive calmness and an order that she could predict. Out of the ordinary was not her desire.

Eva could recall some of her early years. She remembered living far from where she was now; in the countryside, in the quiet. These times had a strong influence on her. She learned well from those that were around here. She learned skills that were not taught where she studied now. Swordplay, bowmanship, and dancing. All of her favourite activities. The activities she hoped would be called into play here. So she could for once excel and exude confidence and enthusiasm.

Quickly she returned to the match in hand when she realised the clanging sound was not a memory but a signal that a goal had been scored. A goal in her own net!

"Eva. What are you doing you stupid waste of space!"

Her captain would likely have used much more colourful descriptions, but standing just behind him was the short but stout referee and deputy headmistress.

"Sorry." Which she didn't mean as she pushed herself from the post and bent down to pick the ball up.

"You should do that more often. Maybe it'll distract our enemy." The captain looked up from Eva's legs and sniggered through a dirty smile.

"In your lonely little dreams, poo-stain!" And she threw the ball with all her effort into his groin. It had the outcome she had wished for. He bent over slightly winded, and with his eagerness slightly bruised.

The team captain stood and composed himself.

"Squeak, squeak little mouse," he jeered. "Go run to your mummy if you want sympathy. Oh, but you can't, can you?"

The majority of her team giggled at their captain's

putdown. The referee did not hear his remarks, nor would probably care if she did.

Eva strutted over to him and without warning nor hesitation, thumped him directly in his throat and followed up with a sharp toe kick between his legs.

"Get your mother to kiss that better, you little pig," Eva spat.

"Eva Ward," the referee shouted. "Apologise now, then get yourself to the Head. I'll be having words with your guardian too."

"Shan't." And she made a hand gesture to them all.

Ward wasn't her real surname but simply described her situation. There were a few other wards in town, primarily abandoned bastards where the parents could not be identified.

Eva stomped off and then began to run to get away from the jeers from the other players. Was it the best-kept secret? She'd not heard actual detail in the rumours, but she'd often thought that some people knew her parentage. Was it just her wishful thinking, that one day, somehow, she would have a family, no matter how lowly they might be?

Eva had another thing going for her, maybe not her ball-kicking ability, unless it was the captain's sack, but she was the prettiest. She didn't know it, but the others did.

When Eva reached the Head's office she paused and considered just running off home. At this moment she didn't care, but underneath, deep down, she didn't want to be in more trouble and did feel that she could eventually learn where she came from.

Hoping not to be heard she knocked very gently, like the little mouse she was described as earlier.

"Enter!" Came a firm call from within the office.

Eva didn't go in. She was considering her options, run or take the punishment, again.

"Enter, quickly. I haven't got all day."

Eva still didn't move, but the door opened just a moment later.

"Oh, Eva. Not again," the Head said softly but despairingly. Evidently, this was a regular occurrence. She put her hand on Eva's shoulder and directed her into the office.

"What was it? A Frog in the head boy's trousers? Worms in Lottie's satchel?" enquired the Head.

Eva was deciding whether to tell a more acceptable story, or whether she should tell the truth.

"I swore at our team captain," she declared. "Then I kicked him in his balls." Always best to tell the truth. Well, most of the time.

The Head listened to Eva's story of how the altercation came to pass. She had listened to many stories, and many from Eva. A slap on the wrist or a smack on the backside didn't seem to make an impact on this headstrong girl.

"Eva dear. I understand how you must feel. But you have to get your head out of the clouds and think about what you are to do with yourself, not dreaming about finding a long, lost family.

"It could be better, or it could be worse. You're not a

bad student, regardless of how many times I see you here, but you need to apply yourself, even when you have little interest."

Eva eyed the cane in the corner of the Head's office. But this time, it was only soft reassuring advice.

Eva was dismissed and left the room, but did not return to lessons, rather she strolled aimlessly home with small tears forming but withholding them well.

The only woman in her life was Annea, her guardian. She was the closest thing to a mother, but that relationship didn't seem to be complete.

Party Time

To provide a contrast to the situation of being under attack from outsiders, Alvar decided to arrange an event of merrymaking, dancing and dining. This would be an occasion open for all to attend, from royalty to the lowest worker in the fields. The target result was that his people would firmly realise that life was indeed first-class with him as King. He drew a list of his selected friends and upper noblemen. His close council were requested to fill any remaining places with businessmen of good standing together with a few of their employees. Not the dross of the gutters, but hard-working, tax-paying folk that such an event would have an influence upon.

Eva had just laid out supper when Annea arrived. A small fire was burning happily in the kitchen grate, and two bowls of steaming stew waited on the table with warm bread. Her mistress had a wide smile on her face and she held several papers close to her chest.

"Is that a secret, or are you going to wear that grin all night long?" Eva asked. Ignoring what had happened earlier in the day, Eva put on a convincing pretence that all was well; just another day.

"No dear, not a secret. But it might be your future," Annea replied hopefully.

"My future? On such a small piece of paper. I hope I have more to look forward to than that!"

Annea laid the papers in front of Eva and sat down at

Soul Thieves

the kitchen table beside her. Eva started to read the top sheet. It was a hand-written list of people from the more well-to-do houses in the city. Eva knew most of the family names. Apart from their status, she recognised another thing that they had in common. They had sons or daughters of her own age.

Before Eva had turned the page Annea had started her supper. Breaking off pieces of the crusty bread and dunking them into the thick gravy.

"This is lovely Eva. Which recipe was it?"

"What? Oh, I made it up."

"You'll make some lucky fellow a wonderful wife."

Eva wasn't listening, deliberately so. She had started her own meal and was reading the second page. It was a design for an invitation. The invitation to Alvar's festivities.

"There's going to be a party?" Eva had always enjoyed such events when she was smaller. Hiding out under the tables with the other children, stealing food, and making a particular nuisance of themselves. In the more recent years, she found them quite irritating and pointless. Excuses for drunken and debauched behaviour.

"Is this the guest list?"

"It's part of the list. Alvar is arranging the noblemen invitations, but I'm preparing this section. And we're both invited. It is my list after all." Annea sat displaying a wide satisfied grin which Eva couldn't understand. Annea knew what she thought of this type of event.

"Well, you can go. I'm washing my hair."

"But you don't know when it is."

"I'm washing it a lot. It gets very dirty on the college fields."

"Come now, Eva. A nice dress. You'll be the prettiest girl there. There'll be fights for your favour."

Eva continued eating, and then she understood. Pretty dress, a ball, eligible young men, Annea's pathetic smile. Annea was trying to suit her, again.

"Well I hope you enjoy yourself, but I'm not going!" Eva stood and pushed her chair back scraping its legs over the stone floor. She stared irately at Annea and walked hastily to her room.

It was one stage in her life that she wanted to put off. She was not ready for relationships, marriage, or bearing children. She wanted to remain, in some ways, a child. No responsibilities.

A few days had passed and the evening of the ball had arrived. The commotion inside and outside of the castle was apparent. Excitement filled the air wherever Eva seemed to go.

Annea was in her room readying herself with her finest clothes and jewellery, whilst Eva sat in her room staring at the dress hanging before her that Annea had spent so much time preparing. She tore her eyes from it and grunted, looking at the floor. "Stupid ball. Stupid dress."

She raised her eyes to the dress once more and sighed.

Alvar's event was well under way and his halls were filling with people from all walks of life. Mingling between classes was encouraged, but the natural order soon became apparent. The working classes, labourers and tradesmen, were quickly snubbed by the noblemen if indeed they attempted any conversation.

The only group of guests that freely mixed were those of the middle classes, shop owners, and employers of other descriptions. The nobles tended to congregate together but still felt the usefulness of integrating, slightly, with those immediately beneath them.

So was the natural class system structured.

The short walk from Annea's rooms to the great hall was quiet as the King's attendants were all busy with preparations in the kitchens or cellars. But she decided to leave the building and re-enter through the main gate, it felt a bit more grand that way.

From her previous employment with King Godwyn, she could recognise a good proportion of the visitors from towns and cities further afield. She hid quietly in the shadows and watched for a moment. When there was a lull in the guests arriving she moved briskly to the door.

Annea entered into the hall and stood atop the small stairs awaiting her announcement to the other guests by a short grey-bearded man to her left. Unlike other guests that preceded her, Annea did not need to offer her an invitation. She was known by most officers in the castle, and the gentleman that stood beside her now was a trusted friend.

"My lords, the lady Annea and lady Eva." Several heads within earshot turned at the announcement, but their gaze bypassed Annea and fell upon Eva standing in her mistress's shadow.

Eva stood as a picture of pure elegance. Dressed in a pale blue velvet gown, open-shouldered with flared cuffs. Her hair was not untidily draped around her face and neck as usual, but tied up in a loose ponytail, leaving a fringe halfway down her forehead and revealing her slim neck and smooth shoulders.

They moved into the main hall as the conversations restarted and accepted drinks from one of the many waiters that were weaving between the revellers.

"Very nice," Alvar remarked in a slow lecherous manner as he stepped from behind the two women after looking them over for a moment.

"Pardon?" Annea became immediately defensive towards his tone.

"It's very nice that you could attend," Alvar added, worming his way out of his unfortunate utterance.

"Thank you for the invitation, my lord." Eva had no idea why she blurted this stupid response, he hadn't invited her. It was surely just an instinctive polite reply.

The small group of minstrels changed their tune to a slow march on Alvar's hand signal. It was one of his favourite melodies.

"May I?" Alvar raised his arm towards Eva who was visibly taken aback. He was the King, a married man. Quite handsome, but a villain.

Without a second's hesitation, Annea moved forward and placed her hand upon his and walked towards the dance area, dragging Alvar behind. Eva was left alone.

"Hello."

Eva turned round but did not reply.

"That was a lucky escape. I hope you'll thank your mother when she returns from her dance."

"She's not my mother." Eva's reply was probably too abrupt considering that the young man was only making polite conversation.

Eva looked again at the fellow. He was holding two glasses. Here we go, thought Eva. This must be the first in a line of suitors that have been set up for me.

"They call me Sel."

"Why, do you work in a shop?" Eva's remark was cruel, but it still brought a smile to the lad's face.

"Ha, no. I think it's because my full name has too many consonants and not enough vowels. People can never get it right."

This boy is either thirsty or too stupid to realise he's holding two glasses. Is he ever going to offer me one Eva thought?

Sel turned to face a petite woman approaching from the direction of the cloakrooms.

"This is my fiancée, Mia," Sel said as the woman joined them.

"And this is?" Sel looked at Eva with raised eyebrows waiting for the introduction.

"Eva."

How selfish and self-centred could she be, thinking that everyone was there for her? She considered the situation and decided to take it for what it was, a simple party. Upon this decision, she relaxed and her body visibly became less tense.

"I'm Eva. That's my guardian I suppose, Annea." She nodded in the direction of Alvar still dancing with Annea.

This couple were obviously from out of town. They were as much alone here as herself, and she wasn't exactly making them welcome.

"I'm sorry I was a bit, rude. But I wasn't really in the mood. Annea keeps encouraging me to meet more, well, young men. I thought, perhaps, that you…"

"Were asked to make your acquaintance," Sel finished her sentence and chuckled. "Just hang around with us. We can have a game without any unwanted attention. If you don't like someone, you can say that I'm your husband."

"And what about me?" Mia asked, slightly annoyed that her new fiancée was marrying another woman.

"Well, we can say that it's ok to have two wives where we come from."

Indeed, over the next hour, as the three sipped wine and watched Annea dancing with the King and conversing with friends, several potential suitors did approach Eva. And of course, none were up to her exacting standards, which were deliberately set so high as to make it impossible to achieve.

Annea strode back to the waiting group, face slightly flushed and with a graceful bounce to her step.

"Ah, you've made a new friend I see."

"Yes," replied Eva. "This is Sel and his fiancée Mia."

Annea's face dropped slightly. "Oh. I noticed you

talking to several other young men too. Some of them are from grand families you know."

"Yes, but they all seemed a little awkward to me, mistress. They must be the remaining sons that they haven't managed to palm off on unsuspecting girls yet. I'm glad you enjoyed yourself though. Shall we go?"

"No, wait. That's one of Ophilya's favourite tunes." Annea heard the melody that the minstrels began to play. It was a jolly tune, and the first one that Annea recognised as being requested by Ophilya.

"If you won't dance with a man, then you can dance with me." She grabbed Eva's wrist and pulled her reluctantly to the floor. Embarrassingly, Eva followed but it was obviously against her wishes.

Annea forced Eva to lead, and she did appear to start enjoying the moment. It was a long time since they acted this way. Probably not since Eva was just becoming a teenager, when they would dance around their home, singing and laughing.

The dance floor was busy, and the music played loudly, but from the main doors, it was apparent that a scuffle was breaking out. Annea could see a few, maybe four or five, burly and untidy men pushing into the revellers. She moved Eva to one side, out of the way and into a position of relative safety.

Alvar stood and watched. The men did appear to be making a line for him, but his guards did not intervene. Almost as if he was expecting this disruption. Ophilya was seated and did not stand to see the commotion.

The infiltrators surged forward as the crowd parted

frightened before them. The man at the centre had a readied bow in his hand, surrounded by his colleagues with drawn swords.

Alvar's face changed and filled with concern. He did not identify the central character with his pointed beard and patched eye. These weren't his men. He took a step back and was stopped by others cowering behind him, looking for leadership.

His guards remained at bay. They were instructed beforehand not to intervene with this show. There was also a distinct lack of volunteers from the audience that were willing to defend their King. None, that really knew Alvar, would want to risk their lives for his safety.

The bearded assailant drew his bowstring taught, aimed at Alvar's chest and loosed the arrow.

Sel, who had been forced to the opposite side of Alvar to that where Annea and Eva stood, lunged forward bearing a silver platter in his hand, grabbed from a waiter standing close by, shattering the glasses to the ground as they fell. He extended his arm and thrust his platter-shield in front of Alvar. The arrow struck its centre and penetrated up to its flight.

Sel continued his dive and crashed into the King's shoulder throwing him to the ground in an undignified sprawl.

Alvar's personal guards were shocked into a quick reaction. This was not the plan for this evening. They forged their way to intercept the attackers, who, although their task had not been successfully accomplished, chose to make a hasty exit from the hall.

The group were chased through the doors and all escaped onto waiting horses except one who was felled by an old man who used the crook of his walking stick to ensnare the man's ankle. He fell with a crash onto a small wooden chair which splintered, and was then pounced upon by the pursuing guards.

Alvar was on his feet again, having been pulled up by Sel. He dusted off his tunic and strode past Sel to where he could see his wife casually eating fruit from her plate, still seated. He steadied himself at her table with both hands and leaned forwards into her face.

"Are you not at all concerned my dear?"

"But why?" she replied quietly for none other to hear. "Were they not part of your entertainment?" She knew they weren't. Not by their direct actions upon her husband, but because they were under her pay. But she attempted to uphold her pretence.

Alvar stood up and with an accusing look at his wife, turned and walked quickly from the hall.

"Get him to the cells." Alvar pointed at the restrained assailant. "We'll soon get to the bottom of this."

As Alvar departed he couldn't help but have a feeling that he knew the bearded bowman. But where from he could not fathom.

Eva led Annea to where Sel stood with Mia close by his side clinging onto his arm. He'd risked his life, possibly saved the King's, and for what?

"What did you expect, a knighthood?" Nothing more needed to be said to explain to Sel what Alvar was really like.

Party Time

She loosened the ponytail from her hair and shook it to let it fall more naturally in its usual straggly form, kicked off her uncomfortable pointy shoes and paced barefoot swiftly home.

Sorceress

Sorcery is not just a flick of a stick and some pseudo-ancient schoolboy mystical incantation. Oh no, it's much deeper and more complicated than that. More like sinking into a sea of souls, navigating into the consciousness of the living, and sometimes the dead. Feeling what your subject is seeing, and seeing what they're feeling. It's mind into mind. There's no trickery that whizzes objects willy-nilly around the room. Of course, that effect can be achieved, but it's only the mere spectators that imagine the magical translations are transpiring, after being put under a drug-induced spell, or some form of fleeting hypnotic trance.

Not to denigrate those conjurers who do manage the odd whiz and bang, for their skills that can blast a man from his horse do have their use. And more so in this age when survival with King Alvar on the throne is a constant menace. That's not magic though, just pure science.

Few have mastered, no, not even mastered, but more dabbled with the control of the human mind. Various fakirs would perform to an unsuspecting crowd, put on a small conjuring show and relieve absent-minded witnesses of the odd coin or two.

But two living souls, in this realm, have a superior knowledge of visiting the depths of the psyche. Neither practices for their own good, and perhaps it is for this reason that their desires have not corrupted their intentions and transformed them into simple thieves.

Annea worked most nights well past the time when the candles had been extinguished in the rest of the palace's chambers. It was far less distracting when lords and ladies were slumbering and restlessly being tormented by the fat that lay in their stomachs; a regular occurrence for those that kowtowed to Alvar's commandments. People are only too willing to say yes in the right places and congratulate Alvar for his thinking and actions of the day, being rewarded with a feast and the tolerance of their King.

There were far too many lords and ladies who'd taken the side of Alvar. Respectable people from not too distant a past, who had earned their people's respect whilst fighting in the good King's campaigns, defending the realm from usurpers, or just managing their estates to best feed the country. But upon the death of the Good King Godwyn, past allegiances would need to remain forgotten, and alliances with the current power holder needed to be made.

Annea carefully selected pungent ingredients, measured and then mixed. Dried herbs and skins of various insects and animals were crushed and ground with liquids in a steady and scrupulously adhered-to recipe. The resultant draft was carefully tested by one of Alvar's attendants. Whilst poisoning Alvar would have some major benefits in the long term, in the shorter term as he'd gasp for breath, he would wreak havoc shouting orders of execution before stumbling to his private chambers to convulse and die, hopefully, in pain. And he was not without his own conjuring tricks that he could swiftly employ as a counter-attack. But a strong poison, concocted to deceive and be undetected, that might be a good strategy.

The prospect of this allowed Annea to continue to provide medicinal beverages for Alvar. But she would have to take much care in the production of such a potion. One slip, the merest hint of a double-cross, and a heavy price would need to be paid. And such a heavy price would normally provide light but brief entertainment for Alvar and his entourage.

But this draft was a mere concoction to alleviate the flatulence Alvar frequently suffered. Perhaps too much good food and wine, especially after the events of the previous day's ball. Whatever the cause, Annea's potions normally hit the spot and Alvar would rest again.

"Annea, my nurse. What would the world be without you to mend my body?"

"Sire, you know that another would take my place. And I wouldn't dare to assume that my attendance to your Highness has any consequence. Have you recovered from your encounter with those thugs last night?" She hated the fawning nature of her own words, none of them said with the least bit of truth or meaning. Alvar wasn't stupid, he was well acquainted with grovelling worms.

"Indeed, and thank you, yes. Many could take your place, but it would take many years before they could earn my trust, and learn my needs and desires.

"Tonight, I have no need to retire, now that I have

taken the sweet nectar that you provide. But I wish for some company. I think you understand my meaning, young female company." He had certainly appeared to have forgotten the attempt on his life.

This wasn't an uncommon request, and Annea would help. Typically she'd have to secure the services of a local girl from the lower cellars, but never anyone that'd ever be likely to wait upon Alvar. Whilst she hated what she was requested to do, she knew that silver coins in the hands of a young victim would be welcome to feed her most likely hungered family.

"Blonde or…" Annea was not fearful for her own well-being, perhaps that of her assistant Eva, and spoke to inform Alvar of her feelings.

"Don't mock me. Go!" He was well aware of her toying tones, but she was still of much use.

Not a time to apologise for her mocking attempt at a question, she bit her lip and backed away. Walking at pace from Alvar's warm chamber, and out into the damp corridor that led to one of several spiral staircases, Annea often wondered how life could've led her to spend, what she assumed to be the rest of her days, serving this tyrant.

Although the old King, Godwyn, was married, he treated Annea as a very close confidant. Godwyn himself was a well-educated and practised sorcerer. During late-night meetings, secrets were shared that no other living soul was party to. She was often referred to as his second wife by sniggering courtiers. Annea knew this and occasionally winked back at the gossiping ladies of lesser importance as she swept past their pathetic gatherings. She instinctively knew it was very wrong, but the feeling of importance, of not being equal but better than others, that was a basic urge that most possessed.

Annea was a young woman when she first began to study at the King's palace. Only later were thick defending walls erected, when the throne changed hands. But it was a splendid and ornate surrounding for her instruction. Every realm, if not every man of importance, had its own mystic, astrologer or seer. And she was being trained to succeed the current ageing incumbent. It was a skilful position to own, and Annea was chosen from rumours of her gift, and her ability to open her mind.

It was once told that Annea was standing in an arched doorway waiting for her tutor to arrive, after purchasing items for the next lesson, when she suddenly, and with great strength, thrust out her arm to restrain a young man walking past her and out into the street. The fellow was taken by surprise and turned to admonish his restrainer when a large crate fell from a winch two storeys above the doorway. Evidently, this deed was interpreted as clairvoyance, but it was not true fortune-telling. Annea simply experienced the panicked labourers' thoughts as they struggled in vain to restrain the load hanging from the gantry. With capabilities such as these, she would be prepared as the next sorceress and be a treasure to the realm.

Many years of reclusive education passed, where Annea would bolt herself into her room to study.

Leading a part hermit-like existence was all the public needed to be told. They came to revere her.

Clairvoyancy, mind reading, and other methods to read and contort the mind were not easily taught. Within a short period of time, she had obtained a level of skill in these fields that surpassed those of her teachers, including the current King's seer. Though still in her twenties, she was becoming to be regarded as somewhat of a freak.

Science of the psyche was only part of her teaching. A greater part was the combinations of ingredients in the production of potions and draughts. Whereas feeling the happiness of a person in the next room by a simple mind trick was a veritable skill, concocting a brew that could float in the breeze like pollen from a spring blossom, or be dispersed in drinking streams, and which could bestow happiness on hundreds, that was much more powerful. And Kings and Queens will always desire power.

By the time Godwyn was evicted from his throne, Annea had too taken an apprentice. Eva was in Annea's care from when she was very small, and she was regarded as more of a mother than a governess. Whilst marriage was almost certainly forfeit when in her position, Annea had dreams of keeping Eva from following in her profession, and wished that one day she would marry and find a caring partner, keeping well away from the dangerous ways of the sorceress. But she was defensive over Eva's acquaintances, and preferred to keep her close to herself, with the almost certainty of a life in solitude.

Eva grew up in the care of Annea and the comfort of Godwyn's palace, not cosseted when a child, but was most definitely restricted in her adventures as she turned into a woman, and kept away from the lustful desires of the palace's young men. Annea had become her keeper and defender, and Eva would have to be protected from all.

Annea had arrived back in her rooms after the recent meeting with Alvar. She walked through her well-stocked library and sat down in a low chair in the adjoining study.

"So, how is mad old Alvar then mistress?" Eva sat at a long narrow desk resting her round chin in the palm of her left hand, her right flicking the nib of a quill over some parchment as she worked on a potion task Annea had set that afternoon.

"Same as ever my dear. Boring, obnoxious, farting old tyrant." They shared a small laugh, and in Eva's sultry smile, Annea could see that she must act. Eva could not fall victim to Alvar's nightly desires and requests. She must take action that would have severe penalties. Alvar could not abuse anyone anymore.

Annea directed Eva to her bed chamber amidst protests that it was not yet late. "You can continue that potion tomorrow. Or we could go into town. Alfred's son is in town, he's a very handsome fellow and you two would be well suited."

"Mistress Annea, please don't keep trying these tricks. I'm not ready to have a boyfriend, a husband, or anything else."

"But it's only natural. Girls get married and have children. That's the way the world works you know."

"Well, you didn't. And you're my mistress, not my mother."

Annea bit her tongue and waited until Eva had broken eye contact. "Oh, very well. I can see we're not getting anywhere with this. Off to bed then, see you in the morning dear." She waved her goodnight as Eva reluctantly left the room.

Annea looked on as the young woman departed. She remained seated until Eva was out of sight, then, with a sigh, stood and moved towards Eva's desk.

The potion task that was set for Eva, although she did not know, was a complicated but extremely useful potion and the task was designed to occupy her for the best part of two days. It was designed to be a love potion, one of the most popular and expensive offerings by travelling chemists. Of course, more often than not, these failed dismally in producing the required results, unless you're keen for your intended girl or boyfriend to have a bright red rash over their face. The unscrupulous vendors were soon hounded out of town. Concocted with the right technique, however, the effects were quite startling. Not just a potion to acquire the affections of the intended victim, but its main function was to subdue conscious thought to enable the implantation of your own will. Enchantress potion number one.

Although Annea had tried over many years of caring for Eva, to dissuade her from learning about potions, sorcery and seeing, she had failed miserably. Eva would nod and agree with anything that Annea suggested, mostly about not becoming a sorceress, and then do completely the opposite, pulling books out of the libraries and reading until late. At least, if it was concocted successfully, this potion would have some use.

Annea waited until the study door closed and then waited for Eva's footsteps, up the narrow stairs to her bedroom, to fade. Now to work.

From a diverse array of pre-prepared ingredients, and some necessary fresh components, Annea meticulously measured and weighed, counted and ground, until a small kettle atop a glowing red grate was steaming steadily from its spout. This recipe wouldn't be found in the books available for Eva to find, nor in a language that others would understand. Special formulae were the trademark of revered old magicians, and were seldom offered to others, unless in exchange for the magician's desire, usually a pocket full of coins. This particular procedure was part of a collection that Godwyn had gathered during his early years on the throne. There was always something in the King's possessions that would fulfil the desires of most beholders of valuable potions. And for those that couldn't be persuaded, the King would employ more convincing means.

Reading the final details of this brew, Annea closed the book and returned it to its place of rest. By morning the task would be complete. The poison would be ready in time for Alvar's breakfast.

Eva was not suspicious of what Annea was up to, for she always called it a day after Eva was asleep for the night. But Eva, although tired of reading and experimenting, wasn't in the slightest bit drowsy, and she climbed the short wooden ladder from the landing outside her bedroom door, and into a dusty attic. The attic had a small square window which was always propped open to air out the damp smells. It was four floors up and overlooked the main gate of the city, where she could observe the ant-like people about their daily and night-time activities.

Beyond the gates were a few small roads and then open fields at present filled with ripening barley. She dreamt of being wild in these open spaces, allowed out of the castle confines which she perceived as a prison-like home. Maybe she could become a traveller vending her restorative beverages and ointments, she certainly didn't want a position like Annea's, to be practically enslaved to a tyrannical ruler.

"Eva sweetheart, have you taken to sleeping with the bats and spiders in the attic now?" Annea was standing atop the ladder which she had climbed when Eva's bed was discovered to be empty. "Come now, it is quite late and we have a small trip planned for tomorrow." Annea did not intend to stay in Abeline after she'd administered her concoction, and had already packed a small bag with necessary items for their journey.

Annea climbed the last few steps into the loft and directed Eva to bed, but she herself stayed in the attic to tidy away some ingredients that were hidden within her robe. Items that would be best not to have discovered.

A floor below Annea's study, and to the south and sunnier side of the castle, Alvar was disturbed by a messenger with rather fascinating intelligence. From the kitchens and local apothecary, two reports were obtained of an elderly woman buying some strange herbs and spices. Items that were rare to use, but insignificant on their own. Together, however, they set alarm bells ringing in the King's head. There wasn't much left in Godwyn's mind that Alvar hadn't extracted before he was disposed of, and the combination of these two purchases could only point to one explanation, poison.

Annea had just put the finishing touches to her concealment, when she heard the sound of large-booted feet kicking in the door of her apartment. She had to descend the ladder quickly to protect Eva, but the men were already climbing the staircase after failing to locate the women on the lower floor of their home. There was no time, Eva would be safe. She is asleep and innocent. Annea retracted the ladder fully into the loft and closed the hatch. Feeling cowardly she squatted quietly on the floor. If she were to descend, then it'd result in her certain capture and death. Eva would be safe, she repeated to herself.

"Sire, she's not here. Only some young woman." The soldier exited Eva's bedroom with his arm firmly around her waist and his hand over her mouth to muffle the screams.

"Then she'll have to do. Either my sorceress will surrender, or an example will be made, innocent woman or not. Let her consider the consequences, and punishment will be tomorrow evening as the sun goes down."

Deception

After the muffled screams of Eva withdrew beyond her room, Annea tentatively descended into the empty apartment. What had been a happy and enjoyable evening together was now deserted of love and homeliness. Annea's previously cool and calm interior was now flustered and confused. She'd thought Eva would've only been awoken and questioned, but still remain safe. Not arrested and carted off and surely to be interrogated.

"What was I thinking? I should've defended her, given myself up or fought them off." Annea thought. But she knew that her instinctive reactions were right. She was just chastising herself for no reason.

She sat down holding her hands tight, trembling. Mulling over events in her mind, rocking back and forth on the small stool, she proposed ideas to herself, then defeated them one by one with rational argument. Her rocking stopped, and her mind became totally in agreement, Jaryd. Uncle Jaryd will know how to settle this quandary.

Jaryd lived in a smallish three-storey house within the castle walls, but far from the centre of the town. He was a middle-aged bachelor, preferring to spend the majority of his time in the company of friends in civilised discussion rather than in the inn for raucous merriment and flirting with the town's wenches. He had once been romantically ensnared, promising his whole world and life to his future partner, but his engagement was so sorrowfully terminated when his love decided upon a foolish path to power, forsaking that which ordinary folk would take satisfaction from.

In his early years, he studied various varieties of herbology, chemistry and medicine, and practised for many years as a doctor, moving to Abeline some twenty years ago.

He had long since given up serving the community as their medical practitioner, partly due to the suspicion some of his prescribed remedies would receive. Jaryd became more reclusive, withdrawing from serving the ailing public, and concentrating his efforts on his main aptitude as seer and sorcerer to kings. This was certainly more rewarding monetarily and the scope of his experimentation was only limited by his imagination and inspired by the requests from his employers.

It was a bright and clear morning as Jaryd set out on his constitutional stroll into the centre of town. The townspeople were setting out their stalls and undertaking early morning chores. They watched questioningly as Jaryd walked past, wondering what test he would be planning, yet none knew what actually transpired behind his closed doors and drapes, nor who the visitors that he seldom received were.

After his several errands had been completed, most accompanied by terse but polite conversation with the storekeepers, Jaryd turned back for home.

He had just turned the final corner on his return journey when he came to a sudden halt in front of a cloaked figure of a woman. Jaryd did not need to lift his gaze from the sandy streets to know who stood before him, for he had felt her presence trailing him since he first left home. Yet he was compelled to look at his stalker.

They both stood emotionless for what felt like an age then threw tight embraces around each other. Clinches of utmost friendship and greeting, but both parties had moved on many, many years ago, and a reuniting of old love this meeting was not.

He stepped back holding both of her hands in his and beamed a most welcome and handsome smile straight into her heart. Jaryd recognized that she was troubled and his suspicions were confirmed by a visible sadness in her eyes.

"Oh Jaryd, I've been oh so foolish." She was not referring to their separation, but to her own recent unwise behaviour.

Jaryd had noticed a heightened level of commotion late the previous night and, through cracks in his shutters, had also observed the bumbling investigators patrolling the streets obviously in search of something or someone. Seeing deeper into Annea's head, he was extracting thoughts which he could correlate with the earlier happenings.

Pulling thoughts from an unprepared subject was child's play for Jaryd, but also a talent that Annea had grown to detest but had learned to prevent, in normal circumstances. With her current state of mind, Jaryd's task was easier to achieve. But this was no time to be standing idly in the streets reminiscing. Annea held his hand tight as she began to stride off in the direction of his house.

The front door appeared unlocked as the pair entered his house into the dim entrance hall. Narrow shafts of light cut through the dusty atmosphere providing the only source of illumination in the room. The heavy pungent air filled her nostrils, but she could still discern the sweet smell of a brewing pot of tea. Jaryd was always a superb master at creating a refreshing drink, possibly due to not using the average leaves that other folk had, but more likely due to his knowledge of unusual herbs and their mildly narcotic effects.

Annea sat down in his small kitchen as he opened a window overlooking a private terrace, to gain more light.

"It has been a long time, but I'm aware that this is not a social visit. Please, what troubles you so?"

"Eva. My dear Eva." She was bravely restraining her distress, nevertheless, her eyes were reddening and tears were starting to form once more.

Jaryd poured a fresh hot cup and presented it to Annea. "Tell me all." He knew this was going to be important, even serious.

Annea explained all that had happened and the reasons why. Her fear for Eva's safety, her stupidity in thinking she could remove Alvar, her inability to defend Eva, and her confusion as to what to do to resolve the situation.

Jaryd sat, relaxed, and admiring the bravery of this lady. Sometimes you have to seize chances when they present themselves, and he wished that he had half of the courage that Annea possessed.

"Please help! Please!" Annea pleaded through streaming tears.

Jaryd remained calm externally, wishing that this would influence Annea who would hopefully quieten down and become less agitated. Within though, his mind was racing. He now knew that his path was being drawn and his life's direction being written. Eva had to be liberated.

A short time passed and Annea's hysteria subdued. The room was quiet.

"Assuming, as you say, that Eva is in danger of losing her life, she'll be confined in the dungeons. From there she cannot be rescued without an army, which I don't have and couldn't raise in a month let alone the day we only have left." Jaryd was describing the options available, and they were few indeed.

"You know Alvar, I know Alvar. If an example is to be made, it's not going to be a slap on the hand or a fine. Eva is going to die without our help. I'm almost certain of that."

"I will take her place. It was my doing," Annea blurted out through a trembling mouth.

"That may well have been a possibility last night, but Alvar's anger will have raged and there will be two lives lost if you go down that route." It was not tactful, but had to be said. Annea knew that the situation had developed purely due to her hasty actions.

"So, logically, if we cannot save her life, we have to let her die."

Annea's face showed rage at Jaryd's indecision, but before she could speak he began to explain, "We have to have meticulous timing, nothing can be left to chance, lest there will be our lives lost too." Jaryd stood and paced slowly next to Annea.

"Alvar is determined to primarily set an example to his opposition. With the killing of a young woman, mothers and fathers of their young hot-headed sons will think twice about supporting their struggle against the tyrant.

"Shortly after her death, her body will be returned, even to you. His anger will have been satisfied, and his lesson taught. He will expect you to become subservient once more."

"But how does that make any difference?" Annea was confused at Jaryd's hopeless plan.

"Well, as incomprehensible as you may believe, I will retrieve her soul. You tend the body, let me do the rest."

That was unexpected and took the breath out of Annea. Naturally, as the sorceress to the King, she had knowledge of men entering into death, and returning, but this was certainly impossible.

"She'll be executed, no, murdered, at sundown, and her soul will quickly dissipate into death and beyond. What you propose is ridiculous, even if you could do what you say, her soul will be long gone." Her tone was angry and blunt.

That was true enough. A person's spirit would linger if it departed its body during the daylight hours, but would quickly succumb to the pull of others at sunset and later.

"Annea, I do know that." He looked at her in the hope to assure her that this was not a crazy plan. "We'll just have to retrieve Eva's soul before the sun goes down. I think that's possible." Jaryd nodded as his plan settled in detail in his mind.

As kings rule the lands of the living, in death too a ruler exists. Not a ruler that shepherds and directs his people, but a supreme ruler that has no consideration for others in his care. This was the current situation in the world where spirits set off to lie in peace. And this person was called Varga, Lord of Souls.

The day passed too slowly for Alvar's liking, He did not care about catching the attempted murderess, and the whole episode was to only serve as a lesson to other would-be assassins. As young as Eva was, and innocent as Alvar knew, she would die that night.

He had eaten a hearty supper and was standing outside of Eva's cell, facing her through the rusty iron bars. She still did not know the reason for her imprisonment, only that it was unfortunate as the King put it.

It was time. Alvar signalled to the jailor and he walked over selecting the correct key from his belt as he went. The lock was undone and the door was pushed open.

Deception

Two guards stepped into the cell and approached the frightened young woman on the floor. They lifted her, one under each arm, and paraded her out of the cell and past Alvar towards a small chamber out of sight of the other prisoners, but not out of sound.

Alvar and the executioner followed closely behind, entered the room and slammed the door securely shut.

Jaryd and Annea had retreated to her apartments which were now void of guards' attention. The main living rooms were in disarray after the guard's fruitless search for herself, but her study was mercifully intact.

They both worked all day and into the late afternoon, forgoing meals and rest. The only aim was to set free Eva's spirit and claim her body.

Jaryd removed his diptych sundial from inside his coat and set it by the window, aligning it precisely. "It's time. There is nothing further we can do now."

The pair exchanged apprehensive glances as Jaryd held her hand tightly.

"If all is well, go and take back Eva's body."

Outside the shadows were starting to lengthen, and Annea proceeded from her rooms and towards the staircases that led to the lower dungeons.

Alvar stood in one corner as the two guards pushed Eva down onto a stained cold stone altar. He peered through the door's hatch into the corridor where the jailor stood. He looked up towards the ceiling and to an iron grill which exited to a small yard at the rear of the castle grounds. The jailer nodded, "Sundown my lord."

"May your soul float quickly, and thence rest in peace."

Eva lay pinned down, still wearing her white nightdress, and defiantly spat into Alvar's face.

"It could've been quick you savage little tramp, but now, this is going to be slow." He signalled to the executioner who was now holding a long knife in both hands.

"May the gods forgive me," he muttered to himself and plunged the knife deep into her chest.

"It was supposed to be slow you fool." Alvar pushed the man aside and stared down at the dying girl.

Her last struggles faded and her head fell back onto the stone. With her peaceful face, closed eyes and wearing her white gown, she'd be easily mistaken for an angel fallen to earth. A small trickle of blood leaked from the corner of her mouth, shattering the angelic illusion.

The triumphant glare of the merciless King's face slowly faded. He stood without remorse staring down at Eva's lifeless body when his moment of satisfaction was interrupted by a thumping on the chamber's door.

Annea was distraught and berating the King over his actions, banging on the door and fighting off the jailer who was attempting to restrain her.

Alvar opened the door and pushed her out of the way.

"If I see you again, I'll kill you," he spoke through tightly gritted teeth. "Now leave this kingdom, and tell your compatriots what dissension will bring." He stormed off ignoring the insults shouted at his departing back.

She turned and ran into the room throwing herself sprawling over Eva's still body, then cradled her head bringing it tight to her chest. Stroking Eva's long hair Annea repeated quietly between irrepressible cries, "Jaryd, please help, please!"

Alvar Spits Feathers

Alvar was resting reasonably content within the main tower's uppermost apartment. Of course, if the captured attacker had survived his questioning long enough to be of any use, then Alvar would be even more pleased.

Surrounded by his generals and guards, he rose from his seat and gazed from the window.

"My Lord," his chief of staff announced. "I am confused. As I look outside at the darkening night, there appear flickers on the horizon. Is my sanity in question? Is there some sorcery here?"

Alvar turned to his officer with a growing realisation that all was not as first thought. Was there truth in his officer's remarks, for he too had witnessed an unusual evening? The sun had indeed set and gone down beyond the city walls, but yet, there was an unusual glow still filling the inner courtyards.

He looked again at the night sky, shaking his head and trying to focus on the world outside, but it was not dark, the sun was still apparent and not yet set.

"What trickery is this?" Alvar shouted. "It is night, but yet the day is still with us. There are people still at work in the distant fields, yet they should have retired and taken their stock to shelter."

The officers crammed to the windows and too realised that things were not as they seemed but an hour earlier. Outside, the night sky grew bright, the sun returned directly from the darkness to set again.

Alvar Spits Feathers

"Get that witch and the girl's body," he spat as he circled the room unable to fully come to terms with what was happening. "And get that bloody wizard too. He knows, he, he cast a bloody spell on me."

The officers and guards stumbled around the room towards the exits, clumsily clashing swords, and shouting orders as they left. "Search the towers, all of the rooms, find them, now! Bring them all back here."

Fuming and puffing like a blacksmith's bellows, the outraged King began to piece together the situation. He had executed Eva hours before sundown so her soul would continue to linger in half-death until it passed to its final rest. Alvar needed her body returned, to use as a guide to recapture her soul.

The search for the missing trio had been in progress for some time, but no sign nor scent was found. Annea's apartment had been overturned searching for clues as to their whereabouts, and the castle and grounds were under constant scrutiny. Jaryd's home too was being investigated, but it was deserted and looked to have been recently cleared out. Empty spaces on his shelves revealed that he was expecting the soldier's presence and had time to prepare to flee.

The lack of any positive news reached Alvar which did little to calm him from his madness. He locked himself in his study and contemplated his next move. Although he could contact his advisors, his seers, but they typically were not favourable to his rule and would likely hinder his search even more.

His only course of action, if he was to secure Eva back into his captivity, was to venture into death himself.

The journey into Varga's realm had never been made by Alvar before; he's not an overly accomplished sorcerer. He had read various ancient and modern accounts of passing into death, and was partly aware of the cautions. His mortal body would be vacant, and his soul would need to pass into death. Failing to maintain a secure path back to life, his body would decompose and his soul would be lost.

Varga had been roaming and ruling the lands of death for many years. He treated them as his own and did not take kindly to trespassers, and there had been many, most of which remained imprisoned in his world to do with as he pleased.

There could be no other reason for the earlier deception, Alvar calculated, than to take the girl's body and soul and reunite them. If that was their intended plan, then Jaryd must've entered into death at least an hour ago, assuming he had found suitable shelter in this world. He would have to move fast.

Alvar's study and store were filled with potions obtained from wise men of the past, the old King Godwyn, and Jaryd too. These would elevate his consciousness and aid his leaving. Adjacent to these mixtures were further smaller containers which held his most entertaining possessions, captured souls of the dead. His enemies, peasants and unwary passing travellers were his main targets. He hadn't the power or knowledge to reduce a man to his component parts, his body and his soul, by himself, but used a palm-sized flask which had been primed for this purpose by Godwyn.

Emptying a soul onto the floor, a merciful act for the long-kept spirit, would show him the path of least resistance into death. This would be a path that he would soon follow, and a path that he must also return.

Alvar sat on the cold stone floor surrounded by his chosen tools. He uncorked the potion bottles, similar to those used by Jaryd and other seers, and wafted their odour around his head. Before breathing in this heady mixture, he prepared the beacon for his return. Used successfully in the past, as documented by others, he needed a link to the living world and chose pain. He positioned a thumbscrew, fixed it to his heavy wooden desk and opened it wide enough to accept his left hand's little finger. These devices were not in short supply in Alvar's rooms, but this was a particularly savage type, with sharpened pins on the inner surfaces.

He tightened down the knurled knobs and the pins gripped tight into his flesh. He winced with pain but continued until droplets of blood formed at each spike's entry into his finger. Alvar wanted to ensure a strong enough connection with his living body when his soul departed.

Lastly, with tears forming in his eyes in pain, he opened his soul bottle and poured it onto the floor watching it pool on the surface before running away into the thinnest gaps between this world and his destination. He breathed in deeply and exhaled. His mind swam in a nauseating swirl. He vomited. A few more breaths and his crossing began.

What Alvar lacked in experience and ability he made up for in determination and persistence. He continued breathing, becoming somewhat drunk on the gasses entering his lungs, but soon his sight in the living world faded and a cold darkness chilled him to the core.

Everybody that entered this world whilst still having a living body experienced it differently. Alvar could not sense the spirits passing by but was shocked at how they manifested themselves as grey swimming figures by his feet. He bent forward and touched a passing figure; he felt nothing. Searching for one soul in this crowd, without any distinguishing features, was going to be a mammoth task.

In all directions that he looked, to his left, right and straight on, there was nothing but darkness and drifting spirits. He felt a tensing in his stomach and a realisation that he had made a dangerous voyage with no hope of success.

"How could this be? What does Jaryd know that enables him to travel here? Perhaps he is lost too." Alvar angered himself by his lack of talent and swore under his breath.

He looked down once more and chose to follow the swimming souls as far as he dare. Desperately Alvar issued commands to his legs but they failed to respond. He was riveted to the spot where he entered this world. The pain pulsing in his finger and hand had bound him between both worlds. Without fully relinquishing his ties with his material form he could not go any further.

With a last-ditch attempt to start his quest, Alvar turned and tugged at his arm, trying to release it physically from the thumbscrew he had attached. But as he looked to where his arm should be, there stood a soul-sweeper, a creature bound to Varga, with his dark hand holding Alvar's arm where it exited this land.

Alvar's feeling for his link with his living body was still present, but fading into the background. His pain was being numbed by a cramp-like rigidity spreading up his arm, aching and throbbing as it neared his torso.

"Pain? You have a little pain?" Alvar thought he heard humour in the voice, but if there was an associated smile, he couldn't see it.

"Just let go. Come with me and rest, eternally with our master."

His numbness spread and tranquillity flooded into his mind as he succumbed to the sweeper's invading power. It was the sweeper's position to collect wayward spirits, but this one appeared warmer than the norm, something which aroused the sweeper's interest further.

There was little that kept Alvar from being totally consumed, but in the moments when his invader paused to savour this soul's warmth Alvar's consciousness woke momentarily and he pulled through the numbness to the pain that remained deep in his hand. His mouth opened and he screamed. The agony rang in his head and the smell of blood was in his nostrils.

He was lying on his floor clutching his left hand tightly, blood seeping between his clenched fingers while the thumbscrew remained closed on his desk, retaining the separated digit.

That was not the most successful of Alvar's exploits, and his failing only angered him and made him more determined to regain Eva under his control. If he had realised that Eva was the key to commanding Annea and perhaps Jaryd too, he would not have despatched her so hastily. With Annea's apparent love for this girl, a word which he was so unaccustomed to using, he could control her and learn from her, become her equal and then her superior. With these powers, Alvar considered that he could be immortal.

Through his continued pain, his mind began to race and work out more plans, filling himself with fantastical dreams.

Jaryd's Voyage

Whilst Jaryd had made the journey to Varga's realm on many occasions, it was not a trivial task. He would have to ensure that his mortal body remained protected throughout the whole process. This was easy to achieve when in his own rooms, but when within chambers in Alvar's palace, which were undergoing a thorough search, this would be a dangerous task.

Jaryd knew that Alvar and his guards would be searching by now, after the deception was lifted and he could see the true state of the evening sky. A chance discovery of his motionless and cold form would be the end of his conjuring days as a free man, although his life would not be taken instantly, working without hope for Alvar would be far worse as Annea could testify.

Annea had led him to a small cellar under the main kitchen areas. This was normally used to keep the waste from meals and their preparation, destined for the pigs the following morning. Annea thought that the smell would deter a full investigation of this room, and had set up an area behind some oak shelves for Jaryd to perform.

Annea stared at Jaryd silently. He was her, and Eva's, only hope. Jaryd was well aware that Eva was her daughter, her only child, and he returned a knowing smile to Annea.

"Please be calm Annea. I will be as swift as I can." Jaryd tried to comfort her, but his words made little difference. Annea knew that hope was all but lost, and

Eva would soon pass completely into death, but she trusted Jaryd too.

Whilst death was just another road for the soul to take, in these times, this journey would be painful. The King was always searching for ways to experiment to control his people. He had taken to extracting the souls from executed prisoners, in order to test out new theories. He even ventured clumsily into death himself to extract the life's last remnants when a suitable subject was not available in the living world. Annea knew that Eva would have a painful existence, and even worse if Alvar managed to hunt and capture her. For she knew this must be his immediate task if he failed to locate Jaryd and herself.

"Hide. I will search you out upon my return. Take care of Eva's body."

Annea glanced once more at Jaryd with an expression of gratefulness. This was a risk that she knew Jaryd would take without question, for they had been close many years before. Many years before the birth of Eva.

She closed the cellar door firmly, and ensured the latch was tightly engaged. Two turns of the key should hold would-be intruders at bay long enough for any attempt at breaking down the oak door to rouse Jaryd. A long bench was then placed across the threshold, and a few sacks of fruit on top of this. She stood back and looked, and hoped, then turned and cautiously exited. The kitchen staff were still busy with the preparation of food, cakes and bread for meals the next day. They did not notice Annea as she made her way out into the lower corridors, and then into a friend's quarters close to her own. These, she hoped, would've been searched first and would now be safe to enter.

Jaryd could enter death's realm easily, but he preferred silence, and the commotion that was evident several floors above was proving a little distracting. He withdrew a small flask from within his grey cloak. It was protected by a green velvet bag which was tied closed. This potion, which was made many years ago, would enable him to raise his mind more quickly to the level required to see and enter death.

He unstoppered the small flask and took a quick sniff of the blue vapour slowly rising from its neck. Holding the container at arm's length he started to breathe deeply. His vision began to cloud and brighten. His surroundings began fading and unfocussed objects started to solidify within his mind. He had his eyes firmly closed now, but still needed to take a small sip from the blue liquid which sat thick and cold at the bottom of the flask.

Bringing the potion nearer, taking one more breath of the thickening vapours, he tipped one, then two small drops into his mouth. He held them there for a few seconds, adjusting to his heightened awareness, before allowing himself to swallow. An action that would completely remove his feeling for this world, and awaken those in the world where he hoped to quickly find Eva.

While Jaryd's body remained completely motionless, no breathing of the stale air, or beating of his heart, his eyes appeared fully open as he looked around the all too familiar surrounding he now found himself in. But he could return quickly and into life once more if the occasion arose, and if he was able.

A living being's soul would enter this domain at the outermost boundary between life and death. This world appeared circular to Jaryd's eyes, although it was perhaps spherical, but more likely, dimensionless. The point of entry wasn't random, but wasn't completely predictable either. There was no exact correlation between the living world of trees, buildings and mountains, and the world Jaryd now occupied. How could there be, there were no landmarks here at all. It was a barren, damp world. Only the small boats that Varga's helpers maintained for extra special deliveries, for kings and queens, for those reluctant to enter death, or those that needed to be returned to life, were visible above the slow ripples of the ground. The gently undulating surface appeared to form a vast peaceful lake, where the banks could not be seen, but this was far from being simply water.

Jaryd would have to make his return to exactly the same spot where he now stood if he hoped to return and occupy his body in the cellar. A miscalculation could lead to an unexpected appearance of his soul far from his actual body. The movement of a soul in the living world was tiresome, and almost impossible. Even to return to the next room, although the physical walls would not be an obstruction, would require extraordinary effort to join up to resume life in full human form.

As any departed life remained in death, it would slowly, at first, embark on its voyage until it reached the outer edge of Varga's own lair. Jaryd collected two small boats and secured them together. This he would use as his homeward journey reference point. A third boat would enable him to travel more swiftly and hopefully gain ground upon his target. He gently entered the craft trying not to create too many waves which could attract Varga, his personal helpers, or angry and confused souls recently embarking on their last voyages. Easing himself onto the central seat, he lifted both oars and set off following the direction of the current.

Jaryd rowed gently, but swiftly, occasionally glancing beside his boat to watch glimmering shapes drift aft. Although the forms were discernible as sleeping humans, they had no substance as such, but confused souls could still perform voluntary motions. An occasional limb protruded above the glimmering surface in a defiant gesture. Not all people were ready to die, and not all souls wanted to be laid to rest. But none could resist the steady flow.

A small arm appeared and its hand rested on the bow of Jaryd's boat. Then it gently slid along the side to sink beneath the surface at the rear. Jaryd estimated that Eva had entered about an hour earlier, but he was making good progress, tiring but steady.

He stopped rowing after about forty minutes, certainly, this must be far enough to have overtaken Eva. He drifted along in the current and concentrated on Eva. He was alone and without any physical guidance, only his thoughts and lingering memories of Eva as he knew her. It was a while since he had been in her presence, many years had passed, and she was not the small child he remembered.

Souls left a trail of memories, a scent in which to follow, as they travelled their final path. The later memories would be the first to be deposited. Jaryd watched keenly as he remembered how Eva used to play with instruments in his and Annea's laboratories. He recalled a time when she would've been about six years old, pretty, and very inquisitive. Would these memories be visible soon?

Many other memories of childhood events were flooding before and around him. It was going to be difficult to filter all of these from those of Eva. Then something took his full attention. A bright green flash and a steady yellow glow were just to his right. The recollection of a dangerous experiment entered his mind, and he proceeded to row closer. Jaryd was drifting at the same speed as this vision, and he could now remember fully what he was seeing. Eva had entered his study carrying a small tube of yellow liquid.

"Uncle Jaryd, I've got a present for you." She held out the tube with the fizzing potion. She dropped it accidentally onto the floor and a flash of green light appeared followed by the smoky shape of a small lizard. A simple parlour trick that most fair magicians could perform, but it was the most significant trick that Eva had ever performed as it acted like a bright beacon for Jaryd.

He was alongside the ghostly shape of a young girl. Eva's womanhood had receded into her youth, and she was now quite easily recognisable as he had remembered many years ago. Leaning over the side, he rolled up both sleeves, not to prevent them from getting wet, but to remove any chance that a spirit might gain any purchase, and placed his arms into the flowing stream. He grasped Eva's wrist and ankle and pulled her swaying figure into his boat. How close was he to Varga's lair, were there any of his minions searching for reluctant occupants of his world?

Jaryd lowered one oar and altered course with his other hand. Eva was wriggling, as a child does when being playfully tickled, and attempting to leave his boat and return to join her sisters and brothers. He had to use the gentle force of his boot to keep her in place, whilst rowing with both arms against the flow of souls. He had rowed backwards on his outward journey, and he had now changed his seating to row forwards, thus counteracting any difference in strength between his arms, for he had to return to the two tied-up boats acting as a marker.

It was quiet, and there was no sign of Varga or his half-dead assistants. "This should be plain sailing," he thought, but could not afford a lapse in his attention to the task in hand. Scanning around the horizon revealed, that although it was quiet, they were not alone. A silhouetted cloaked outline was evident, but its course did not indicate that it had noticed the soul thief, and for this he was grateful. These servants could row quickly when required, and the noise created by the splashing oars would only serve to alert others in the area, and maybe Varga himself, for he'd be only too keen to discover a living being in his lands.

An unshod foot rose up before him and then disappeared. An old foot, which indicated that they must be close to the edge. Then a face loomed before him, with its gaze focused on him in a deathly stare. This was a recent addition to Varga's population, and it appeared not to want to remain. Both arms were flung up and over the bow, and the creature lifted itself up, burbling incoherently. Whilst this was not a direct danger to the mission, the trail left by this soul would entice others to follow, and soon they would be overwhelmed with passengers all wanting a journey back home. Now that would be like rowing a fishing boat with its nets out, and progress would be slow if at all.

Jaryd raised an oar and pushed firmly into the chest of the new occupant. It stood up to its full height with an astonished look on its face and fell backwards, but not without releasing an ear-piercing screech followed by a hefty splash. This would certainly attract other souls to his position, and, worse still, the attention of death's helpers. He returned the oar to its rowlock and increased his stroke. Eva was ageing and now looked much older and was no longer attempting to escape. She was the image of a striking young woman, in her early twenties, with long straggly wavy dark hair. Full features on her face were not discernible, but it was evident that she was beautiful.

In the distance, the deathly inhabitant made a sharp turn towards the commotion surrounding the boat and

Jaryd's Voyage

its fugitives. Jaryd noticed spray spewing from the tips of its oars as they stuck hard into the ground full of fleeing spirits. There was no point keeping quiet now. He let rip with all the force that he could gather. Every last scrap of effort that lay deep within him was brought out of reserve and used to power themselves towards their escape. Shrieks came flooding across the lake, and others were returned from every point. Varga would himself be hustling in for the capture and kill.

In the darkness to their immediate right, a small craft came hurtling with breakneck speed into the path of Jaryd's ferry. Two arms thrust forward to grasp hold of Jaryd. He parried them with his right boot, and then swung his oar out from its rest and across the face of this demon. The oar struck home and the demon swayed but regained balance to lunge again at the fleeing couple. Jaryd stuck both oars down and gave a single almighty heave, and the craft stopped dead. The pursuer's lunge missed by an inch, and the sorcerer levered his oar on the gunwale and under the attacking boat. It toppled, but the demon counterbalanced. The return toppling, however, overthrew the cloaked fiend and he struck the water, only to resurface alongside the next moment. He grabbed the front of Jaryd's boat and failure appeared imminent.

Eva's features were more apparent as Jaryd gazed at her in a deathly enchantment. All of Eva's memories had now departed her and the images that remained swirling around her could only be from what is yet to come, the future. Jaryd could not interpret this, but he knew that

that didn't matter. The fact that memories of Eva's future were present meant there was still hope, hope for Eva at least.

Two more arms appeared over the edge of the boat, followed by another, and another. However, these were not the cloaked hands of denizens of this world, but from spirits of the very recently departed. Those that still had some small fraction of consciousness. Those that still declined to accept that they had embarked upon their last voyage, and they were determined that the demon would not take them. Three, four, or five pairs of emaciated arms clambered and enveloped the puzzled demon. He was not a match for the multitude of assailants, and could not resist their pulling him under the surface.

Jaryd looked swiftly around, disorientated by the events. He caught sight of the two moored boats a short distance ahead, well within reach in a few minutes. His boat was being swamped by spirits wishing to use it as a means of escape, so he had no choice but to lift Eva into his arms and alight from the craft, for the final steps would have to be made without the protection the small vessel afforded him. He sank to his knees' depth, but was easily capable of walking. The spirits paid no interest in him, except for the quizzical look and recognition of a living being in this forsaken land.

As Jaryd arrived at his entry point into this world, a cold painful cry struck him from behind. He turned and caught sight of Varga nearing fast. Quickly, Jaryd turned to depart this world and return to his own. A searing hot pain hit him between his shoulders and he cried out and fell forward, stunned and disabled.

"Your life is over. Your soul is mine, to taunt or trade as my will desires." Varga loomed closer.

Cleriks and Alvar

Since the time when man first walked the Earth, their spirit, their soul, the essence of their being which differentiated one from the other, and all from the rest of the Earth's living creatures, was created at birth and travelled within the living body until death.

At birth, the human soul is cast. The ability to perform deeds for the good of others is decided here. Conversely, the option to do the opposite is another of the choices that are set.

But, this is not a black-and-white situation. Between the extremities, all shades of personalities are created, and during the body's maturing, the soul grows too. The goodness can make way for the bad, and vice versa.

The person's upbringing, teaching, and bestowed love are all aspects that decide the manner in which the hidden soul matures. A genetic disadvantage of embarking into life with a soul towards the dark end of the spectrum, can, to some extent, be guided to the more acceptable end.

The existence of human nature, essentially the state of one's soul, had been accepted from when communities of men settled together. For millennia, gods were created and destroyed, both the light and the dark. Men and women wanted to understand, but comprehension of the workings of a man's spirit eluded them.

Only within the last one thousand years did the existence of the soul and its destiny after death be recognised, and then, only by a few. These select men and women studied, meditated, and altered their consciousness to leave the living world and visit the departed spirits.

In time, these men, given the name cleriks, would collectively maintain the two distinct worlds in death. Although they did not directly control these worlds, the ability was theirs to decide the destination of the good and the bad. Gates into these afterworlds could be opened and closed, filtering the souls into the correct locations.

It was their belief that the soul would either be dissolved into oblivion, or let join the mass of others in total joy, to exist beyond death, in love and contentment, for eternity.

Belief was important for man. A belief that a person's conduct through life would determine his fate was a powerful weapon that could be used to control a land's people.

The door into the darkness was easily traversed by those who left the living world completely and voluntarily. Travelling was still with danger. With a living body still in life, the soul was not permanently at rest here. But to overstay a visit could still lead to passing beyond the point of no return and the dissolving of one's spirit to disperse into nothing.

The ability to enter into the light was not recorded

accurately. Cleriks had tried, but their souls never returned. Their bodies in life would live until they slowly decayed. Whether entering into light was a total destruction of the spirit, or whether it was the start of complete and total satisfaction was not known. The established belief was for the latter, and that was what was taught.

After a time, the clerik's power and control grew. The resentment of this power, and its perceived abuse brought anger to the people. The majority of the population was being treated as less important citizens, with a lower value. Inevitably, they revolted. The organisation of the cleriks was dismantled, and the major cleriks were banished. Minor cleriks were encouraged to stay, but now under the control of the state, controlled by the King. Belief was undeniably a worthy foundation.

Varga was such a clerik. He had left the clerik organisation before the remainder were banished far from the lands that they practised within, and had been the main instigator of the direction that the clerik order followed. He was young but very talented, and one of a very few that were able to enter death completely and wander freely.

After the effective dissolution, he alone tried to assassinate the King, but his attempt was thwarted and he was later executed. Before his death, with full knowledge that his soul would be directed to the dark areas, he slipped from the living world and forcibly took the path to the light. Not excited by the beauty and calmness of this place, he returned and successfully shut this space from further residents. Varga had closed the gates to heaven.

Jaryd was raised by major-clerik parents, but their untimely deaths at the hands of those that swore to hunt down all such previous members of the order, forced Jaryd to travel far from his home. He settled as a traveller and sorcerer in Abeline and was soon in the service of King Godwyn. He knew little of the workings of the defunct order, but had learnt much from his parents. He had ventured into death long before he came of age, and his experience became known, revered and respected, although he himself chose a quieter life as a semi-recluse.

The minor-clerik council existed from the banishment to the present day. These cleriks were present in small numbers in most major cities and towns. Abeline itself had eight members in its council. With the control that their order once commanded gone, they had reverted to spreading the belief in a blissful afterlife.

As had been the case for many centuries, the councils were ruled and controlled by the monarch, currently Alvar. But they were not happy with the state of affairs in the world of death, for they were well aware that, even though they preached belief in heaven, the only path open to the dead was under the dark rule of Varga.

A year or so earlier, and unusually for Alvar, he was attempting to relax with his wife in a small lounge off of his main reception room. Furnished with low recliners, rug-covered floors, and tapestries hanging from the walls with candleholders between them illuminating the room and its occupants in a soft but flickering yellow glow. This room was the ideal place to escape from matters of state and recent events.

He was reclining on a chair with his arms lying beside him, palms upturned, trying to force his anger and stress out of his body and through his arms down to his fingertips. Ophilya knelt next to him trying to soothe him with gentle strokes of his hair and temples. Certainly, this was not a common sight in the castle, and it was obvious, perhaps not to Alvar at this moment, that Ophilya was scheming.

"Alvar. Why don't you have a talk with the clerik council? Maybe they will have more success in finding that girl's soul." This was a comment designed only to belittle Alvar as he had failed so recently.

"Oh, so a bunch of weirdo priests are better than me?"

"No, of course not. But they have more experience, and if they were to try, and die, there'd be less for you to worry about." This went some way to get back into his good books.

Alvar considered the possibility of reducing the clerik council numbers, and maybe even recapturing Eva. "An interesting thought. Summon the council if you'd be so kind."

Just as he'd finished his sentence a knock came to his chamber's door. The council members waited in the corridors at the request of Ophilya some hours earlier. She had a certain ability to persuade the King to do as she wished, without him apparently realising that he was being manipulated.

Not suspecting who was seeking an audience, Alvar walked through his rooms to the door and briskly opened it. He was surprised to see four grey-cloaked men of the clerik order standing, hoods removed, in front of him, and was visibly shaken by their presence.

Ophilya played him as a fool, but Alvar was far from being one of those. He knew that the order's arrival at this hour of the night was not some supernatural summoning, but that Ophilya had constructed this meeting, and instilled the idea in his mind as one of his own. He couldn't understand what she was up to, but that'd wait for later.

Alvar stood aside and two of the four men entered whilst the remaining cleriks waited outside either side of the doorway.

"How can we help?" Such a simple question, but the way it was spoken immediately made the cleriks appear superior to Alvar.

He didn't want help. He never wanted help. But, this time, he came straight to the point. "There is someone I need you to get for me."

"You have soldiers, and guards. Why do you need us?"

"Someone from death."

"But shouldn't this soul be left to rest now?"

"It was an accident," Alvar explained. "She needs to

be brought back."

The cleriks could possibly perform this duty, but they had their own agenda.

"And in return, what do we receive?"

Alvar was not a bargaining sort of man. When he wanted something, he got it. But this situation was different. These men were not going to be threatened by death if they would not comply.

"Go on, give me a clue. Would you like money, a bigger prayer house, what?"

"They are of no consequence. The gates to the light within death are closed." The clerik assumed that Alvar was aware of this, even though they did not preach this to the public.

Alvar raised his eyebrows but knew full well what the situation was.

"We need help to reopen them."

The King knew he had not the skills to do this, and he knew that the cleriks were aware of his abilities too. So how did these cleriks think that he could help?

The tallest clerik stood and faced Alvar, still seated. "We don't have the power to do this, else we wouldn't be here. You lack the required power too." Nothing like putting Alvar in his place, but he stayed calm and seated. "We, all of us, need to defeat Varga."

"And he's just going to come wandering over and give himself up, is he? Or do you suggest," Alvar paused. He looked between the two men, and understood for the first time what they really wanted him to do.

"Defeat him in death." The cleriks confirmed Alvar's

assumption.

"You're all raving mad! You want me to go into death, which will likely be a one-way journey, defeat Varga, which will be extremely unlikely, open the gates, return here, and we all live happily ever after?" He didn't know whether to punch the clerik in the face or wait calmly for his reply.

There was an expectant pause. Ophilya didn't know how to force Alvar's hand. She wanted rid of him. She always wanted to be queen, and not some wife of a lunatic. She had accompanied him this far, and helped him attain the throne, now it was time for her succession.

She walked a few paces and stood close to Alvar, then turned him around so neither of their faces could be seen and their voices unheard.

"Go with them, let them help return that girl's soul, then return here quickly. If they have the strength, then if they open the gates all will be well." Ophilya was still trying for the kill. "Everyone wins."

Alvar waited for some quiet after Ophilya had finished speaking. He looked her in the face and turned to face the cleriks.

"Good luck in your forthcoming clash with Varga." Alvar walked to the door, opened it, and ushered his guests out. "There is nothing more to be said." He raised his hand as the clerik opened his mouth to speak.

Alvar signalled to his guards that the council was leaving.

Ophilya went swiftly to caution Alvar and grabbed his arm.

"You're making a big mistake. This could be your time of glory."

"The door's still open. Why don't you take the glory?"

She threw his arm down in anger, partly because she regarded him as a coward, but mainly due to her own failings in not convincing him to risk all. Then she pushed past him and hurriedly followed the council members down the corridor and out of the castle.

Annea, Eva and Jaryd

Jaryd's essence emerged into the living world, but not into his mortal body. He was a few yards short, and he could see his still body upright where he'd departed. If he had not been hunted in Varga's world, he would've returned easily to the exact location before re-entering into life. But that was not an option available to him at this time.

In his present unearthly guise, these last few yards appeared like a marathon. He contorted his spirit and set forth a wispy tendril of his essence directed at his body's feet. Movement outside of the storeroom attracted his attention. He'd have to be quick, but more disturbing was a small draft of air being pushed under the locked door. An insignificant occurrence, but sufficient for his feelers to become misdirected.

Eva's soul too was ebbing away from his grasp. The soul is like a mirror. Smash it, but each remaining smaller piece still returns a full image. Keep reducing the fragments to smaller and smaller parts, and soon there's just dust, which will melt away. As Jaryd remained in this shape, he felt like he was being pulverised and ground into nothing.

Jaryd's continued efforts made progress until, at last, the pointed end of one tendril touched the surface of his booted foot. It squirmed and flicked up, over his leather laces, and under the leg of his breeches. With a small darting stab, it connected and penetrated his flesh. The feeler began to enlarge like a snake devouring its prey. Soon, the connection had enlarged to an extent that it was now larger than Jaryd himself, and the remains of his soul were pulled into their owner, returning him to life.

He collapsed to the floor in sheer exhaustion, both mental and physical. All of his six senses were in complete disarray, sounds outside the room reverberated and echoed in his head, making it throb and buzz in confusion. The whole room was spinning as after a heavy night on the King's mead. Nothing was coherent. His sense of the dead, their souls and memories, was absent. He knew and understood nothing.

This was a similar state of affairs every time he returned, but much more disordered on this occasion, exacerbated by the decay of his soul whilst outside of his body. He bent forward and placed his palms on the cold floor, lowered his head, and breathed deeply. He needed to return to a fuller state of consciousness before Eva could be restored.

Slowly the spinning contents of the store settled, and double images came into proper focus. The noises from the scuffling outside became clear, and Jaryd was shocked into full alertness following a loud thump on the only door.

"Open this door now! Unlock it or I'll have it smashed through." That was clear enough for Jaryd. The guard's search had reached his place of concealment, but this was the only door, the only exit, and it was barred by guardsmen.

"I'm sorry. I, I can't find the key. It's not normally

locked," replied the kitchen head. There was a sound of a crumpled body crashing into a wooden chair. Annea had obviously taken the key, or hidden it, and the kitchen worker had suffered for it.

The guard captain shouted orders to at least three others. "Draw your swords, use your axe. Open that damn door!"

How could Jaryd have come so far, through death with Eva's liberated soul, back into his body, and yet be defeated now? He glanced around the room, searching for another means of escape. Nothing. Some small crates that would not conceal his bulk, and it wasn't exactly the most sensible of places to hide. He drew in a deep breath, exhaled sharply, and then pulled his longsword from its sheath. Strictly speaking, his weapon was a bastard sword, not two-handed and heavy. It was a shade shorter with a thinner but wider edge, easier to use in confined combat. He raised it ceremoniously to his forehead with the grip in his right hand, and the pommel in his left.

He was prepared and ready for the door to break and the enemy to fall in. The axe-man would be out of the fight as his battle axe's head may still be embedded in the door near the lock. The two swordsmen and the captain would be taken by surprise as he ran through the doorway. He should at least be able to fell one, and then there'd be one remaining and the captain who, hopefully, has his sword still sheathed. Jaryd stood his ground and waited.

The axe-man wielded his axe and struck the door many times during the attack, with splinters of oak flying out from the cut by the lock. The door's defence began to yield, and it was now not long until it would fail. One final swinging blow, followed by a shoulder charge from a guard, and the door flung open crashing against crates of rotting fruit stacked inside. The first guard stumbled into the store, followed swiftly by the second and the captain at the back, all three with swords raised.

The four armed men stood in the centre of the room forming a small circle. They all searched the room with probing eyes, darting from one dark corner to the next, hoping to seek out the three fugitives.

"Flippin' waste of time that was. Right lads, on to the kitchen pantries then we'll go to the mess and call it a night." The captain and his men were a little disgruntled at having to work into the evening. None of them being career soldiers, and mostly conscripts from various workhouses and farms, they'd be more at home with simpler duties than doing fighting practise or terrorising the innocent people of the local villages. But more and more, Alvar's fighting forces comprised recruits that didn't have their hearts in the soldiering profession. There were, however, more dedicated elite forces that were the direct opposite of these four men, forces comprising mercenaries and veterans from lands and wars from far afield. These would not retire so easily in the search for Jaryd and his companions.

Jaryd stood in a dim and dusty delivery yard. His sword was re-sheathed and hidden under his cloak. He knelt down and slotted the shaft of a nearby besom through the iron hoop of the trapdoor at his feet, securing the hatch tightly from would-be followers.

His place of refuge and temporary imprisonment wasn't always a slops room. It stood in the old part of the castle, adjacent to the kitchens and close to the small banqueting hall. It had originally been a store for the King's mead and spirits, hence the need for the locked oak door. But the kitchen's smells were not appreciated by Alvar, so the recent castle's expansion provided more distant halls for relaxation.

He slipped out of sight into the shadows beside a low haystack, and withdrew a flat metal flask from his inner jacket. Eva's soul was residing within his own, not combined with, but separate. And it had to be stored in a safer place else it would dissolve into his own experiences with a surge of energy. The prepared container was opened and offered up to his chest. Jaryd pushed and a dull silvery-grey glowing figure emerged from near his heart and poured into the neck of the flask, growing brighter as it completed its transference. Quickly Jaryd replaced the screw lid and secured it back by his side. Now to find Annea. The castle is not safe this night and they must all leave.

With Eva's soul now held safely, Jaryd walked cautiously through the grounds and entered the castle through an unoccupied sentry post. He was a regular visitor to the castle when Godwyn was on the throne, less so now with his brother sitting unwelcome in his stead. The castle was becoming quiet, as the search widened outside of the battlements, so Jaryd had a far easier task to enter Annea's apartment.

He approached the door, but it was hanging on its hinges. Annea would not have taken refuge there. He could not sense any person's presence here either, but was drawn along the corridor to a door which seemed to be attracting his attention like a magnet to cold steel.

He knocked on the door lightly. There was no reply, no sounds from within that he could perceive. The rusty latch felt familiar in his grasp. It wasn't locked, and he pushed the door half open. He peered inside, into the gloomy space, then entered and closed the door gently.

This was confusing, but he began to understand. He could certainly not see any presence here, nor hear any movement. But there was a definite odour that was already sensed that day, and mingled together with a fragrance which would not be present without the woman he gave it to. A smile appeared on his lips and spread to his face, and he turned to face the strongest source of the perfume.

Annea's image appeared as the brew's effect wore off, and she stood to greet him with a returned welcoming smile. A true sorceress indeed.

The pair embraced without hesitation, holding firm and relieved that each other was safe. Jaryd recalled the perfume he gave as a gift many years ago. An experiment that he and Eva undertook for Annea's birthday. It was an enjoyable afternoon spent in Annea's own study, Eva standing on a low stool, testing the pungency of each ingredient that was added to the small cooking pot. Of course, not everything that Eva selected as an ingredient ended up in the mix. Certain objects, dead crickets and small mice, would not create a welcome fragrance. Only the tried and tested ingredients, and perhaps one or two secretly deposited by Eva, finished up in the elegant glass spray bottle.

Annea stood back and grabbed hold of his sleeve then pulled him into the bedroom. She strode over to the bed and sat down beside Eva's cooling corpse. There was blood on her vest that Annea was now trying to dab clean.

"We cannot awaken her in this state. She cannot know of her own death." They were both concerned that Eva would be unable to comprehend her very recent past happenings. Of course, other people had been resurrected, normally through experimentation where the subject was temporarily put to death to have their soul replaced immediately, but they all succumbed to mental disorders and spent the remainder of their years in asylums.

"Remove her clothes and wash her body. I'll wait in your sitting room." Jaryd hesitated and then turned and exited to room to give them some privacy. He waited for a few minutes, patiently, staring out at the strawberry-red sunset darkening on the horizon. A half moon was already high in the sky, and easily providing enough light to travel by. Annea softly called his name, and Jaryd returned to see Eva laying as if asleep dressed in pale brown leather trousers and a short-sleeved shirt, buttoned high enough to prevent her stitched wounds from being visible.

Jaryd removed the warm canister and held it for Annea to see. The warmth was not provided by his own body, but by the unsettled contents within. Carefully, it was opened close to Eva, and the contents poured directly into her body through her slightly open mouth. The fundamental part of the young woman's existence shone a deep red as it warmed still further in her throat, and then melted into her being.

The two spectators stood silently, watched and waited for some signs of triumph. Jaryd knew, he could feel, that Eva's soul was captured within her body. It had not dissipated elsewhere.

What seemed like an eternity passed, and then, Eva opened both eyes, looked straight at Annea and rolled over to sleep.

Oh how all three refugees needed to sleep in the warmth and comfort, but the pair recognised the desperate need to make a quick and quiet departure far from this evil place, and without further delay. Annea squatted down on her haunches and caressed her cheek and long soft dark hair. Sadly, she had to wake Eva.

"Sweetie, time to get up. Eva? Come on now. We have a long journey ahead." Annea's kindly words, spoken so softly, stirred Eva from her shallow slumber. "We're going to visit some old friends, where we can live safely. Look! Jaryd is here too."

Eva sat up and glanced toward him. She wasn't shy, but she didn't want to linger on his eyes. It was many years since they were last in the presence of one another, probably at Godwyn's funeral service. She remembered his kind eyes, and the striking features of his face. He still had that silly little beard, she thought, and remembered how they had played after she tried, and half succeeded, in removing it whilst he was napping. This brought a subtle smile to her round lips, which unintentionally was directed at Jaryd.

She blushed slightly and took her eyes from his then jumped from the bed, and slipped her cold feet into a pair of waiting ankle-high boots. Jaryd and Annea were equipped and waiting to depart, and she offered Eva a long coat for the cold autumn journey ahead. Eva slipped it on and reached over to a small set of drawers to retrieve a pair of blades that she recognised as hers; short daggers with a stiletto retracted into the pommel. She pushed them into niches in her belt, accessible but secure should they be needed hurriedly. Lastly, she wrapped an old woollen scarf twice around her neck, a gift she remembers that Godwyn gave her before she was a teenager.

All three runaways made swift progress through the castle corridors and chambers, and came to the grand foyer, the last room between themselves and the open grounds. Eva started to ask a question but Jaryd quickly raised his fingers to her lips.

"Quiet! It will be guarded, but not heavily as there are many other minor exits that will keep the castle keepers occupied. I'll go first."

Jaryd crept slowly into the room and out of the safety of the shadows, looking thoroughly for any signs of movement, flickers of candlelight, or approaching footsteps. It was all clear, and he beckoned to his friends to follow.

They had no choice but to cross the centre floor under a crystal chandelier. Jaryd drew his sword as they moved promptly into the open, then into flight toward the exit.

They were in full stride when Annea screamed as an archer loosed his shot and hit her square between her shoulders. Jaryd released a small side knife which was accurately directed at the assailant. It sought its target and buried itself in his upper throat. Annea staggered a couple of short steps on the uneven cobbles, leant to her right and rested upright against the cool corridor wall. The bolt had entered deep into her back, and she felt the blood warmth of her damp shirt down to her waist.

Jaryd and Eva halted steadying each other with outstretched arms, and turned to find Annea sitting on her haunches. She raised an arm and opened wide her palm. Eva rushed back but Jaryd forced her to stop and pushed her aside. He stepped back towards Annea, keeping watch for other bowmen, and knelt in front of her.

"Take it for Eva." Her voice was shaky and quiet. She offered Jaryd a small silver oval locket in the form of a pentagonal medallion on a long chain. It still retained the warmth of her chest where it hung moments before.

Jaryd did not attempt to lift Annea. They both knew the consequence of doing so. He took the locket and secretly secured it in his breeches. There will be time later to explain this to Eva.

"Go! Protect her!" Annea pleaded, as her head dropped forward onto Jaryd's chest. He felt her soul reluctantly depart, and helped it on its way quickly out of reach, then waited to ensure that her soul made a successful departure and mingled untraceable with hoards of others departing this world. Alvar will not capture this one.

After all of her memories have left this world, he placed her gently onto the floor and kissed her cheek. He stood and turned to find Eva staring down at Annea's lifeless shape curled up on the floor. Eva had tears streaming down her white cheeks, and her lips were curled in grief.

"Not now, please. Say goodbye quickly, we have to go now. We'll grieve shortly."

Eva collapsed onto Annea's still body, throwing her arms around her head and back and then sobbing uncontrollably. Jaryd put a hand under her arm and raised her reluctantly from the ground, pulled her trembling body towards his and held her shoulders firmly. She sank her face into his shirt where her tears left their signs of her love for Annea. "I'm sorry, we must leave now."

Jaryd held her tightly for a moment longer then pushed her to arm's length to see a brave young woman lift her chin and wipe her tears on the back of her hand and sleeve. She never knew of her parents or what became of them, but her feelings inside were as she'd expected to have for the loss of one.

He started to move towards the open door at the far end of the corridor, holding Eva's hand gently but firmly, and pulling to persuade her to leave. Eva followed but turned her head and looked over her shoulder one last time. She turned back to face Jaryd, then looked forward and ran, Jaryd right beside her.

Ophilya and the Cleriks

Early evening rain had quietened the streets leading to the main square in Abeline. The usual noise and business were scarce and Ophilya chose her moment carefully to leave the castle and walk quickly, hooded against the storm, out of the grounds and into darkness.

The only light that shone fell upon her face from a small lantern that she had recently lit and held close to her body as she walked crouched. The shadows her features cast over her face would make her unrecognisable to any that she may meet.

After a short distance, beyond the visibility of the main gates, she stepped into the outskirts of a small wood and a short distance later emerged into view of a gathering of cloaked figures.

The canopy of trees held the falling rain from their clothes as they stood silently waiting for their invited guest. Wearing a darker cloak than his fellows and carrying a long crooked staff, the central figure stepped forward to greet Ophilya and lowered his cowl.

"My lady. Thank you for agreeing to this meeting." Haram, the leader, bowed low to Ophilya.

"There is no reason to bow to me, my friend." She smiled directly at him and offered both arms for a closer greeting.

Haram embraced the Queen but refrained from kissing here, too many eyes.

"That wasn't a very successful meeting earlier was it?"

Ophilya referred to the time when she tried to convince her husband to destroy Varga.

"Indeed. It was not according to our plan. But perhaps it is for the best."

"How so?" Ophilya asked.

"There is nothing certain in life, and far less so in death. Alvar may have actually been victorious, and then where would that leave us?"

That was true enough. The people gathered in the woods wanted rid of Alvar, but their plan could quite easily have backfired leaving her husband with immense power and control.

"What is the situation in Varga's realm?"

"We do not have free roam there. Varga has many minions patrolling, we can make only brief visits.

"It has been a busy period. Eva, then Jaryd, and finally your husband have all been visitors, and Varga is displeased with these invasions."

None of this was unexpected, and infuriating Varga would only make her plans harder to achieve.

"Our numbers are small and inexperienced. The state, under the direction of your husband, does not allow us the freedom to teach our ways. If we could educate and train our pupils in the methods that can be used to exit from life and into death, then we would surely build a force capable of Varga's defeat."

"And my husband's too no doubt."

"But we are forbidden these teachings, and are only allowed to inform about life after death in heaven. Not about life after death in hell. Assassinations have been tried without success too."

Ophilya could see that the cleriks' hands were tied, but they could still have a use to her. Without an alternative plan, Ophilya decided that it was time to reveal the only way forward as she saw it.

"We have to use machines. They are not detectable by seers or anyone else that professes to feel the presence of souls. These devices could get close to Alvar."

"But they are just toys. Unnatural creations with no thought." Haram was not easy with Ophilya's fondness for modern sciences.

"They are just metal, springs and wheels. You should not be afraid."

"They are soulless and have their own motion. How can you say that people should not be afraid?" People are happy with living beings, horses, mules, and cows walking. They were warm and had feelings. They had souls. But machines that moved? That was wrong.

Ophilya stared into Haram's eyes. "They don't naturally have a soul, but they could."

"You're confusing me. What do you mean?"

"With an enslaved, confined and hidden spirit, these mechanical devices could not only move, but move with intent. Miniature undetectable assassins filled with a purpose."

Haram took a step away from Ophilya, obviously repulsed at her suggestion.

"You cannot take a soul and put it into a machine. That's hideous," Haram protested. "And the soul would still be detected."

"Not if the soul is encased in the metal machine. It should remain undetectable. And the person from whence the soul came, is already dead. What does it matter?"

"And the dead man's soul has a right to rest, and rest in peace."

"Are you saying that all souls that enter Varga's realm rest happily in death?"

This was a question that both Ophilya and Haram knew the answer to. But what was best, the dead to be tormented by Varga or enslaved by Ophilya?

The pair stood quietly with Ophilya trying to silently convince him to help acquire what she needed. The look in Ophilya's eyes was offering a reward to Haram, if he did as she asked. Haram was like a small child being tempted by sweets, he could not refuse. The machines were her toys, and Haram fell into that category too.

Varga in his Lair

Varga wandered amongst his many captured souls all resting in chest-like containers kept closely around his lair. There were special places set aside for exceptional people, and Jaryd would've filled one nicely.

During Jaryd's visit, Varga was only made aware of the true nature of the invader when one of his sweepers began to close in on him as he was fleeing. The message the sweeper sent to his master was an exciting message of an encounter with a powerful living soul.

Of course, Varga could directly feel trespassers into his realm, or that which he deemed to be his, but there were so many people paying him visits that he had not the patience to try and capture them all. A few had been restrained from leaving and disposed of, letting their mortal bodies wither. Cleriks mainly, but the occasional dabbler in death had also fallen prey.

Jaryd, on the other hand, would not have been disposed of so quickly. His soul would take a special place next to old kings and queens. Unfortunately, and to Varga's disappointment, Godwyn was not one of his special guests. But Jaryd's talent for walking with the dead clearly made it difficult to track him or even distinguish him from a legitimate resident.

Varga only just failed to capture his soul, but had certainly got a measure of his opponent and a taste of his essence. He would be easier to detect next time should he be foolish enough to attempt such a journey.

Varga had waited patiently after Jaryd's escape. Perhaps he had inflicted a mortal blow that would stop him from reoccupying his body, but he had not seen his soul return to his realm. Either Jaryd had escaped unharmed or he had slipped past Varga's watch.

Then there was Alvar. He knew what his presence felt like; much the same as his brother's, but not a soul he wanted to keep, yet. Alvar would be much more use in the living world, who else could sustain the high flow rate of spirits entering into death for Varga to feed upon?

Varga had watched as his sweeper confronted Alvar. It was most amusing and he could see that Alvar was inflicting damage to his real body back in life. But he wanted to test his abilities, so he let the sweeper continue his menacing. He felt no regret when Alvar left his domain, as he knew they would meet again, soon.

But by far his greatest loss was that of Godwyn's soul. When he died, or rather, when he was discarded by his brother, Varga felt his spiritual presence immediately as it neared his world and sprinted to intercept him as he travelled.

Godwyn was a knowledgeable person, had experimented with seeing into death, and was very much an equal of Jaryd in that respect, although he had far less direct experience of the actual travelling beyond the living world. Godwyn was taught by both Annea and Jaryd, and he also had instruction from some cleriks. All in all, he understood Varga's realm.

But Varga was too slow to make this capture. The King's spirit had moved with determination and control.

Varga in his Lair

It knew its intentions and would not be distracted. Varga's barred gate to the light within death was opened by Godwyn as easily as tearing a piece of parchment. Godwyn evaded capture.

Alas, that was not the end of Varga's embarrassment. Godwyn held a passage open in the gate, and a tunnel was left between himself and the living world. Varga, not knowing the function or purpose of this tunnel, desperately struggled to block its path, but the force and heat that surrounded it defeated his every attempt. Through this tunnel Godwyn managed to pass an embodiment of his experiences and knowledge, a duplicate of his spirit. This parcel of hope flowed to one he loved above all others. Then the tunnel collapsed and the gate's opening faded shut.

The only consolation Varga had was that the recipient of this message could not wield its power in the living world. This second soul would lie dormant but safe in its new host. Its power could only be awakened when all ties to the living world were broken and then only by someone who bestowed unconditional love upon another in the same manner as the gift was given.

But who had received this Varga pondered. Not Annea. Although well known as the King's mistress, she had already passed his way without event. And not Godwyn's wife either, she died many years before he did, and they had no children either.

Varga was fearful of losing his authority, and that was a trait he shared with Alvar. Varga's command of his dominion was acquired during his death. He was not

Soul Thieves

always an evil character, but had once been a clerik, trying to serve his fellow men.

After Varga's death and departure from the living world, he continued his efforts of investigating and analysing the two worlds, the light and the dark. It had fascinated many men for so many years, and this fascination burned in his mind. Varga would do the unthinkable. Whereas his fellow content spirits in paradise remained ignorant of the darker worlds, he would venture to this place. Here, his cravings were satisfied. Everyone was equal in heaven, but in hell, his hell, he could rule.

His transitions between these two places continued as he built knowledge and confidence, and then he left heaven and settled to rule in hell. Not wanting to be challenged by his equals or torn from his new home, he closed the gates to heaven firmly with as much evil and depraved spirits as he could muster, the resultant gathering at the gates acting as a magnet, repelling any stray spirit into his own lands.

But what was happening now? Varga could not fathom the significance of both Jaryd and Alvar visiting his dominion, and within such a short space of time. What was Alvar searching, badly, for? For him to take the risk in death, his quest must surely be of great significance. And whose soul did Jaryd steal from him? Varga thought there was a familiarity in that soul. He could still feel the echoes of it being taken from him.

Eva

The fleeing couple trotted slowly on two stolen mares through the castle gates. Their departure was sudden and only basic supplies had been stowed in their saddlebags. The guardsmen did not pay any attention, even though all of Alvar's soldiers were on high alert. But how could they recognise what appeared to be two old beggars, adorned by rags, tottering past on some old mules which had obviously seen many years of service and maltreatment?

This time, the deception was a small example of what Eva had learned from her mother over the last decade. A potion's scent wafted on the air, filling the guards' nostrils with a heady mixture, and muddling their senses. Some settling words spoken softly from the lips of the mounted apprentice, and eye contact with a calming gaze. These were the basic tricks of the enchantress, and with time, they would be performed without the need for the potion's assistance.

Without the use of magic, the hearts of many a man and woman had been enchanted by Eva. The sweetness of her deeds, and the purity of her heart and mind, always managed to attain the friendship of the ladies in the palace, and several of the adolescent scullery boys too.

Once, before she entered into her teens, she'd rushed from her duties to stand and watch the local farmers set up stalls outside the castle walls. These events were a welcome distraction to her studies.

Outside, it was a hectic menagerie of sheep, calves and chickens, and Eva was always thrilled by the bustling excitement on market days. Clucking in cages or being tethered to the wheels of the laden carts, Eva looked at the animals with a certain sadness, but knowing full well what their destiny was and would be.

A clattering noise made Eva turn to see traders and market visitors quickly making way for the approach of a coach and four dappled horses. In the lively market close to where Eva stood, a small cage fell from a low wooden crate and cracked open onto the dusty ground. Two small leverets struggled out and jumped onto the road. Eva, without hesitation, flung herself down and covered the frightened animals with her own body and coat. She curled up and waited for the inevitable stomp of the horses' hooves.

"Whoa! Whoa! Steady on there," the driver commanded his fine mares.

Two footmen leapt angrily down and one approached Eva leaving the other to survey the crowd.

"Get up you stupid girl! This is urgent business, I've got a good mind to have you…" Eva looked up and stared at the young man grasping her hood and pulling to remove her from his path. Her quivering half-smile and innocent stare immediately reduced the footman to an apologetic servant, only too happy to help the young Eva to her feet and out of harm's way. She stood aside, onto the path with the other onlookers. The coach proceeded at a quickened pace, and the two frightened creatures were snatched back and put back in their hastily mended cage for sale.

Just one of the countless selfless deeds that Eva managed to regularly perform. Deeds that earned her respect from most of the King's servants, and many of the noblemen too. Were it not for her standing, being a simple servant herself, several lords would've considered her as a potential suitor to their own heirs.

Now, as Eva rode alongside Jaryd, he could see that physically this was no timid little girl. She had certainly grown up into most people's imagination of what an enchantress would be. Not a little child anymore, not physically, but within her heart, mind and soul, she was the same in nature as she ever was; a delightful companion on this long journey.

"Eva, do you know where we're going?" Jaryd enquired. Not just to enter into idle conversation, but he did want to see what she knew of recent events.

"We travel to Wodel, to seek refuge and assistance from Marcus. He will help us won't he, my lord?"

"He may. He may need convincing. But please, please don't enchant him. His will must be persuaded, if it really needs to be, by natural means," Jaryd replied. "And, my name is Jaryd. I am no lord or yours, no lord at all."

There was an uneasy silence for the next mile or two. Neither knew whether their questions were appropriate. A startled thrush flew from the hedgerow to Eva's right, and darted in front of both horses. The horses continued without alarm. They had been trained as soldiers' mounts, and were quite prepared for events in battle, and would not be troubled by a small bird.

Eva broke the silence with another question, "Was my mistress bad?"

"No child, no. She was the most loyal and kind lady you'd ever wish to call your friend. She tended to you and protected you for most of your life. There was not a day that went by without her kind words falling into a conversation about you, what you did, and what you were doing."

"But if she wasn't bad, why is she not here now?" Sadness crept into her voice and eyes. Although she had many friends, she felt very much alone. She rode on, but looked sideways at Jaryd for some comforting reply.

Jaryd wanted to talk to her about the event with the conjured lizard, but could not think how to evade the questions that would follow, which surely lead to Eva finding out that she had in fact been rescued from Varga earlier that night. He did not want to put himself forward as some glamorous hero, he was more suited to living his life far in the background where he could remain undiscovered, uninterrupted, free. But he had to reply to her question, he could see her distressed state and wanted to bring some more cheerful smiles to her face.

"Eva, what would you do if you were sitting quietly in your favourite and most expensive armchair, studying and learning from a unique ancient text, and a small dirty child runs in holding a quite substantial amount of worms freshly dug from the wet earth? But not just holding these creatures, letting them fall slowly from their grubby palm, and onto the priceless document?"

Eva did not hesitate in answering, although she could

see, after she spoke, where this was leading. "I'd be annoyed, and the imp would certainly know she'd done wrong." Eva was quite certain that the imp in question was herself.

"Annea was far more tolerant than that. On several occasions, as retold by Annea herself, you were that small child. She had not one iota of cruelty in her body, and in that particular instance she merely recaptured the squirming worms, returned them to a small glass jar, looked up above her half-moon glasses, and gently smiled before letting out a quiet giggle."

Eva was settled by the story and the thoughts of her and Annea playing when she was younger. Many events came flooding back as she tried hard to remember. Annea loved her, and took care of her, as if she were her own kin.

They rode steadily on past the shores of North Lake which was on the outer borders of Alvar's realm, and the source of water for the town. Night had long since fallen, and there was now little chance of them making the comfort and safety of the Old Billet inn, where they'd hope to rest and have a much-needed meal.

"We'll set camp just beyond that small rising, off the beaten track." Although Jaryd did not expect any travellers at this hour, he still wanted to remain inconspicuous. "I have a little food that will banish our hunger pangs until dawn, but there'll be no hearty breakfast to see us through the morning."

Eva dismounted with a small stumble. They were both tired and in need of both mental and physical rest.

She unsaddled the horses and led them to a small stream beyond a narrow gap in the gorse. When tied securely she returned to Jaryd to be greeted by a small but gratefully warm fire, upon which a pot was starting to boil. She could smell the infusion filling the air, and the lift that gave her was most welcome.

They were both lying sprawled out on the ground staring into the night sky. The earlier clouds had cleared, and it was now a still and very dark night, with a myriad of stars shining down upon them. Save for an occasional screech of an owl calling its mate, or a scampering rustle for cover of a small rodent, there was complete silence.

Jaryd sat up and lifted the boiling pot from its support, then filled two small tin beakers with the warm drink. He offered one to Eva who was very nearly asleep. She accepted it gratefully and took a small reviving sip. It was sweet and pungent and obviously, the herbs used in its brewing were from a recipe that Jaryd had used before as it had an effect that flooded the mind with awareness. It was a clever concoction that prolonged one's state of alertness and made your heart pound into life.

Was this really what Eva needed when she so much longed to sleep and forget the day's events? She looked hard at Jaryd, although his gaze was at the red embers of the fire. She always remembered him with fondness, and the thought crossed her mind about what sort of a husband he would make, or had made. She did not know if he was or had ever been married, but perhaps her thoughts were just exaggerated by the drink, the romantic setting under the stars, or that she'd been working on a love potion just a short while ago. Anyway, surely he was too old, yet, perhaps not?

"Silly girlish thoughts," she said to herself, then blanked those thoughts from her mind and took another sip. It was hot and made her throat and chest burn when she swallowed. Instinctively she brought a hand to her chest. It felt a little strange and somewhat painful to touch. Jaryd notice her actions and the confused look on her face. She seemed to be quite alert now, and there were things she needed to know, and this moment appeared to be as good a time as any for an explanation.

"Eva, I think it's time that I explained something that has happened to you, but you have no knowledge of." This was going to be complicated, but the necessity to say it was compelling.

"Last night, you were arrested by Alvar, not for something you had done, but in frustration for his own shortcomings. For some reason, he extracted his anger upon you and you were hurt, that's the pain you seem to be feeling in your chest now." Jaryd was not ready to tell her what Annea had been planning, Eva would remember soon enough.

Eva looked down and unfastened the top three buttons. She looked at the small slit on her white skin, it was still weeping a little blood. "I, I don't remember this. How, why?"

"You rested in a deep sleep after the ordeal." He could not assemble the courage to tell his companion that she had actually been dead. "And Annea, with a little help from myself, released you from Alvar's imprisonment. Your wound was tended, and we decided to flee. Consequently, here we are."

"I do want to remember what happened, but the memories don't come." She recalled Annea's death and tears were beginning to form again. Eva would take a long time to grieve over her guardian, companion, and friend. "Please can you help me?"

"Ah, your memories will draw closer, in time. Talk to me whenever you need to, about anything." Jaryd paused and then reached into his pocket.

"Annea wanted me to give you this." He held the small locket-medallion in his palm close to his body and then stretched out his arm to offer it to Eva.

She recognised it immediately. Annea had always said that Eva could have it when she passed away, but this was too soon for her.

"I believe it's a locket and can be opened by some magic. I'm sure you'll work it out, but I reckon it's just an old piece of jewellery." Jaryd did not like to use the word 'magic', but he knew that Eva would understand him.

Eva rotated and flipped it over in her hands. It did seem to be just an old medallion with a small inscription on the reverse, *To my dear daughter*. She assumed this was a gift from Annea's mother when she was a small child. It was certainly very old and the only charm that Annea ever wore, and Eva loved it so.

"And apart from the medallion, the only other request from Annea was that I was to take care of you. Which, of course, I will willingly undertake."

"Thank you Uncle Jaryd, but I am quite able to…"

"And I'm sure you'll respect your mistress's last request." Jaryd looked sternly but comfortingly at Eva, until she replied with a small smile.

"Eva, Annea died tonight because of the desperate efforts of Alvar to increase his knowledge on all matters related to sorcery, and to rule the thoughts of others. He mistakenly believed that he can learn these abilities using theft, deception and trade. He cannot. Certain abilities are required that he will never possess whilst his demand for power is forefront in his life," Jaryd lectured.

"There is good and there is evil, and not much that separates them. Individuals are defined by their actions, and their actions define which category that person will fit into. The homeless vagrant that rests in another's house uninvited is not evil, whilst the owner of the house who evicts the man onto the street is not good. Most can tell the difference," he continued, but did not wait for a reply or questions.

"You, and Annea before you, and Godwyn before that, are well acquainted with the science of creating potions and other concoctions, and in the art of their usefulness. You are fortunate to have been taught by a loving teacher, even though her wish was for you not to become what she was. Power, and the knowledge that you have is truly powerful, can corrupt even the strongest of wills. Annea was no saint, she had strayed from the total path of righteousness, but was always aware of her actions."

Eva began to look uncomfortable as her one true friend's character was being illustrated. But she had not the energy to defend Annea, and was intently listening to every word from Jaryd.

"These potions can control the mind indirectly with appropriate use, but there are other ways that can control and even see within your target's psyche. Your mind and thoughts and what determines your deeds are all enclosed within what we refer to as your living soul. And this soul continues on after the body it contains fails in this world.

"The resting place of your soul is either in, what our spiritual scholars call, hell or heaven. These places exist and not just in the sermons of priests and cleriks that you will have listened to week after week. For centuries, and probably since man and woman walked the surface of this nurturing planet, these kingdoms were without rulers. All equal and loving in heaven, and in turmoil and purgatory in hell. Alas, the gates to heaven have been shut and the path to hell is the only route from this place. All of this was brought about by the rise to power of one that was both evil and good, Varga."

Jaryd's explanations were creating compelling questions in Eva's mind. Who is or was Varga, how can he be both good and bad, how was heaven closed, where is Annea now? The last question was particularly disturbing as she had always hoped that they'd be together in heaven after their life on earth was done, as was told to her by Annea herself.

"To add to this, all souls can be taken from life and

death. But only by ones with sufficient capability, and normally with specific instruments. Alvar has possession of certain instruments that enable him to achieve this feat, and some ability gained from Godwyn that allows him to see into people's heads."

Jaryd thought about withholding some essential details, but decided that Eva was ready to learn who he was. "I too have the ability to see, to retrieve or take undefended souls, and to venture where souls rest. The use of these talents is not without risk, a serious peril of death or worse.

"A healthy living body is a most precious entity, and almost impermeable to control by another. Take care of your body, exercise your mind, and learn to see.

"I'm sorry if I've bored you with my ramblings, but I have to enlighten you with details that you must understand. You probably knew most, or had deduced as much without asking Annea for explanations. Now, lesson one, rest!"

Eva pulled her coat tightly around her shoulders and lay on the ground, lowered her gaze away from Jaryd and watched the warm glow of the dying fire while clutching the medallion around her neck closely.

He too drew his cloak snugly and lay back to sleep. Jaryd however, continued to watch the flickers of light casting delicate shadows on Eva's face, then slept.

Alvar's Unsuccessful Search

When Ophilya heard of her husband's injury, it was quite obvious something was amiss by the sounds and whimpers of agony erupting from his rooms, she, being the ever dutiful wife, rushed to his aid.

Alvar was seated with his left hand tightly wrapped with a small soft towel and clasped by his right. A small patch of red marked his mistake.

Ophilya noticed the thumbscrew with its prize embedded in its jaws still fixed where Alvar had left it, gently weeping blood onto his desk. She walked hastily to her husband's side, knelt, and looked around the room in a fake examination.

"There's nobody else here, so I guess that's yours." She pointed at his lost finger.

"This isn't a time for joking about woman. Do something!"

"You need a surgeon. I hear the cleriks have wonderful doctors in their numbers. My sewing skills declined when I married you dear."

"Don't mention those damn cleriks. Where did they go anyway?" Alvar's mind focused on his wife and her interest in this group.

"I thought you said don't mention them."

"Right now, I want you to stick my finger on. Then you can tell me what they're up to." Alvar was losing his patience and the red stain through the towel was obviously getting bigger.

Alvar's Unsuccessful Search

After several minutes of moans and cries of pain, together with curses directed at his wife, Alvar was finally resting with his hand bandaged after Ophilya had stitched the open stump skin together, discarding the lost finger which was beyond her abilities to re-attach.

"So, this bunch of no-good cleriks, where have they gone?"

"As much as I tried to convince them that we would be really grateful for their help, they departed. Still in Abeline though." But without their distinctive clothing, they would melt into the background and stay hidden. There was no organised state-funded moral teaching in Abeline since Alvar took the throne. The cleriks worked, as any other man, for a living.

"I knew they'd be no help." Of course, it was only Alvar's handling of the situation that meant that he was more or less alone in his search.

"Yes, dear. If you say so," Ophilya agreed, placating her husband. "Looks like you'll have to find your fugitives on your own."

She stood and tidied the small medical chest as two of his generals strode into the room. She then exited to allow them to talk in private.

"Both Jaryd and Eva have fled sire. The main gates are all secured and all passers are thoroughly searched."

"And are all of your guards educated in sorcery and its defence?" Ophilya made a wise choice in leaving the room as Alvar's anger started to grow.

"No sire, but they are both very recognisable," the guard explained.

The colour of the air was rent with expletives spewed from Alvar's mouth. It was not really the guard's fault, they had not been told of the possibility of witchcraft being used. Alvar breathed deeply and calmed down.

"And Annea, you have her?" She needed punishment but was of little importance thereafter.

"Dead sire. Shot when escaping. But we have her body."

"And her soul? That would be more important."

"No. Apparently, Jaryd stayed with her to safeguard its passage. It has gone."

It was little consolation, but consolation nonetheless. Something that Alvar could brighten his day with as nothing else had gone his way so far.

Ophilya's Plans

Ophilya was resting on a small reclining chair in the ornate sitting room in her, and her husband's apartments within the castle. This was normally a very quiet location and was located at the far end of a long corridor that served the sleeping rooms. Tonight, she could not relax, but had thoughts bouncing around in her head. The King was fuming. He had received his first defeat during his reign, and had vowed that to be his last.

Ophilya ensured that she kept her distance from Alvar, not that she would ever voluntarily be close to him anyway, unless there was some advantage to herself in the form of gold, toys or power. She found peace here, Alvar would still be storming around his studies, commanding his officers, or taking revenge on his captors in the dungeons.

Surely Alvar would calm down soon, or would there be an outright war against the culprits that initially seemed to have humiliated him? A contingency plan had to be made in the unlikely event that a new king will replace the old.

Standing just short of her six-foot husband, Ophilya was a picture of elegance, far too well-dressed and graceful than he deserved. But she had her reasons for being his queen, not least the wealth, and the ability to learn and discover the new sciences. Sadly though, friends were lost, and new ones, real ones, were difficult to acquire.

"Ah well. Whatever will be will be," she murmured to herself.

This lonely woman was surrounded by bookcases and cabinets displaying a vast array of her toys. The toys which were laughed at by her husband, and despised by the clergy. However, she understood the abilities and power that these devices had, and perhaps how they could be used, especially in her future plans.

There were no modern inventors and practitioners of these new sciences within the castle grounds, or in the near vicinity, but Ophilya knew the dealers to approach to acquire more machines. Most folk were reluctant to accept that the new tools did not contain elements of the devil. They certainly believed they were unnatural, but, on the contrary, these were mostly just using newly discovered forces of nature, perhaps with the odd exception.

Of course, the folk of Abeline and its neighbours were familiar with the simplest of all machines, the wheel. But a spring-driven wheel attached to a cart that could propel itself without the need for a horse was considered to be very much alien to their world. A child pulling a wheeled toy was one thing, but a toy pulling a child!

Ophilya first became aware of these forms of machines on her first visits as queen to the far reaches of their lands. These trips were successful and brought new trade links with lands from across the seas. The lands' traders introduced her to some small inventions, but it was apparent to Ophilya that this was only the tip of a

Ophilya's Plans

very interesting iceberg.

The commerce was good. Fine cloth, food, and unusual animals were the majority of the cargo exchanged. Ophilya had her own packages delivered though, and these were kept hidden from all others.

In Abeline though, the steady sciences of brewing potions, or attempting to cast spells like fairground magicians, or even the old hermit-like soothsayers predicting the future, were all accepted as ordinary happenings. The new ones employing clockwork mechanisms, electrical charges, or magnetism, were well beyond comprehension.

Ophilya knew that a self-moving clockwork toy isn't going to be the basis for a wealthy future, or indeed lead to unimaginable power. But the same device instilled with the soul of a man or animal, that, perhaps, had some potential. This is where Alvar's collection might be of use to herself.

She walked over to a set of braided pull-cords, and gave a sharp tug on a carefully chosen tassel, then waited. A brief moment later the doors were opened and an old couple entered into the room, greeted the queen with the necessary bow, and stepped closer for her instructions. The couple had been loyal and long-serving attendants, butler and maid, to the old King. Ophilya had sort of adopted them when he was deposed, and shown them compassion after Alvar decided to make a completely fresh start within the new kingdom. She had saved them from death or exile, but her outward showing of compassion was more illusionary than genuine. These people would serve well, and could be of benefit.

"The King needs time and no diversions as he plans his immediate actions. Please, don't be wary of my friends," as she pointed around the room. "I need you to collect them together and set them gently into a large travelling chest. We will visit my sister, I think she needs some company. Make any preparations you need. We leave as soon as you've packed. Oh, and do not mention this to my husband." Ophilya didn't have a sister that the couple were aware of, but had no reason to suspect an ulterior motive.

The Queen left the couple together cautiously removing the delicate items from their shelves and placing them, wrapped in cotton sheets, into the deep chest. She walked the length of the corridor and turned the corner to approach the door to Alvar's main study. Resting her ear against the warm wooden door, she listened intently for any signs of her husband from within. There was no sound. The door wasn't locked, and made little noise as she pushed it open just far enough to squeeze through. Ophilya double-checked that the room was vacant and strode quickly to a smaller door that led to his store room. This was usually locked, and for good reason, it was the place where Alvar's retained souls were held in their unnatural state.

There was little that Ophilya didn't know about her husband's activities and supposed secrets. The key always hung from the picture hook behind his own portrait, a present from herself to him on the first anniversary of his reign. Correct. She lifted the portrait

Ophilya's Plans

carefully from its hangings, and took the key into her right hand. The key fitted into the oval cut-out but did not turn. She tried again in the opposite direction, and the lock engaged. It was open all the time. Strange! Nonetheless, she opened the door and entered the small and stuffy room.

She was wearing a royal green evening gown with deep side pockets, each filled with un-spun wool which would protect her stolen items. Standing in front of a collection of ampules, canisters, stoppered bottles, and jars, she had no idea which items would be most suitable for her future plans.

The sealed glass bulbs were filled with various coloured mists. No inkling as to what they contained, but obviously of some use, she pocketed two and rearranged the remainder so as not to look like there was an empty space.

Pure copper canisters were the majority of the containers remaining. She knew that the reddish-brown coloured metal was a favourite of those that dabbled in adventure with the departed. Apparently, the taste of the metal to the free soul was sufficient to keep the entity in a single shape and within the walls of the container. Again, a couple of these would see her right. She picked two of the medium-sized ones in each hand, they were cold to the touch and she felt a strange and electric tingle travel up both arms. She dropped these a little too sharply into her pocket, and they clinked on the wrapped ampules, but fortunately did not break.

Once more what was left was equally spaced to

conceal any missing items. Moving a step to her right, she stood in front of the largest number of containers, glass jars with tight-fitting lead lids. Nothing was marked or labelled in any way that made it at all clear to Ophilya what the contents were, but she did assume the copper containers held the most precious substances, it being a far rarer metal.

She stood back and looked over the shelves once more, nothing sprung to mind as out of place or attracted her attention, and turned towards the door.

"I'm not sure your husband would be pleased to lose so many of his collection." The voice came from a heavily built soldier sitting in a dark corner. He stood to make himself recognisable in the dimly lit room, and as his features came into view, Ophilya identified him as Alvar's closest advisor. Not so much one of his military elite, but a strategist and counsellor.

"And I don't suppose he'd be too pleased if he knew you were snooping about in his private chambers either," she retorted. "What are you doing here?" She went on the offensive. This was as much her province as it was Alvar's.

"Well, your majesty. After the incidents earlier, I thought that perhaps the perpetrator and their associates would consider it an opportune moment for more deception and burglary. Seeing as the King would be busy with his investigations, they'd have pretty much a free run of the inner castle chambers, nobody would think to search here."

"Except you, it would seem," she interrupted.

Ophilya's Plans

"Indeed. And to further complicate your situation, you were observed on your nightly meeting with your cloaked brethren. Stealing from your husband is one thing, but infidelity, with them! Seems to me that we'll be getting another queen."

His sword was already in his hand by his side, ready for any necessary action, although it was most likely not needed against a single undefended woman. He pointed his sword in the direction of the door and signalled for her to leave.

"After you, my lady. It'll be interesting to see what sort of a tale my lord's devoted wife can concoct before we find him. Oh, and probably best to leave the evidence in your pockets."

Her immediate plans of escape were in disarray. She had no defence or power against the wrath of her husband. From all of the panicking thoughts that were flooding her mind, the only scheme that solidified was to run. The key was still in the lock, and perhaps her swifter body would enable her to get through the door first.

Ophilya had a small greenish-coloured glass jar in her hand, which she threw at her captor in an attempt to delay him. With his right hand occupied with his weapon, he brought up his left to meet the jar where it impacted with a clunk against his chest-plate. He fumbled with the round object which had become slippery with condensation, and it fell from his grasp and onto the stone floor. It smashed at once upon contact, and they both saw that the reason for the glass colour was not the material itself, but the object within.

Soul Thieves

Ophilya was at the door when she heard the breaking glass and the tinkling sound of the fragments as they scattered across the floor, but didn't stop in her escape. Reaching the door first, she slammed it tightly shut and turned the key. There was no expected swearing or thumping at the door from within, but there wasn't going to be time to study this situation, her assailant would break through soon enough. She ran, and directed her thoughts back to her prior arrangement to meet Hector and his wife outside.

Within Alvar's store, the soldier was fixed rigidly to the spot. The green gaseous content of the jar which had spilt irregularly just seconds earlier was taking a more defined shape, not identifiable as human or animal, but certainly had more structure, a glowing core and a wispy outer covering. The cold spirit-like form moved towards the warmth that was in the man and penetrated his clothes, armour and flesh. His muscles tightened in spasm, and his fingers became flexed and then contracted into fists as he was occupied by this force. A human scream of pain and terror filled the air, before the sound turned into the howl of a wild dog. As the cries quietened, the white soul of the human was pushed out from its former body. It hung in the air still retaining a human-like form, and then sank slowly to the ground to disperse into the floor. The physical body now occupied by a foreign spirit, could not cope with the new chemistry and crumpled lifeless next to where it was seated moments previously.

Ophilya heard the cries from Alvar's quarters as she

pulled the door shut, and continued her hurried flight. Returning to her own rooms, she found them deserted. Pulling a warm overcoat from a stand next to the door, she took a momentary look around for anything else that would be of some use in her looming self-exile, closed her door and leisurely continued, trying to regain some composure more befitting of the Queen.

Hector was waiting in the small courtyard a few yards from the main square and thoroughfare of the castle. His wife and Ophilya's chest were already onboard the carriage, and there was a driver at the reins of two sturdy shires. Several other cases were stowed atop the carriage, containing clothes and other personal belongings of the departing trio.

"As quickly as you can please!" Ophilya commanded Hector. She boarded the coach and Hector raised the steps and closed the door, joining the driver on the front bench.

Morning Fight

Jaryd awoke first the following morning and decided to let Eva sleep as much as she needed. The previous day was extraordinarily tiring, and they'd both need to retain as much strength as possible for today's ride to Wodel.

It was a typical chilly autumn morning but the surrounding trees provided some lessening of the cold. Woodland creatures had arisen much earlier than himself and were already busying themselves foraging and feeding. However, not much of the forest food would be compatible with these two. They'd have to make do with what was hastily packed the night before, a little water, bread and dried meat.

The campfire had long since gone out and the smouldering embers let ribbons of smoke ripple vertically upward to be dispersed only upon reaching the canopy above. He broke camp, covered the extinguished fire with loose earth, and packed his bags ready to strap onto his horse.

Eva turned over and stared into empty space, not yet completely awake. She'd slept well but it was time to make way.

"Time to get up sleepy head." Jaryd was waiting with their horses that had spent the night tethered next to the stream. At least they seemed to have had a decent breakfast as they continued to munch on dry grass.

Eva ignored Jaryd's comment and pulled her cloak higher as the chilled air bit at her nose, but she continued to watch Jaryd standing and waiting.

Jaryd had never been in this situation before, acting as a parent, and he was unsure whether he should just pull Eva's cloak away or wait until she saw the need to arise by herself. He settled on the latter, and stood firm, quiet and waited.

"Oh very well." She stood up, letting her covers fall, and pulled on her boots. "Five minutes." She walked past Jaryd to the stream.

She wasn't angry and had a typical Eva smile on her face. There wasn't much that disturbed her as she nearly always saw the good in everything and everybody, perhaps with one recent notable exception.

A short while later, Eva marched past a patiently standing Jaryd, with water dripping from her face and hands, grabbed her cloak and took her reins. "Are you ready?" she asked.

Mid-morning approached as the pair rode slowly out from the forest and into the open marshland, but trying to keep to a more firm track. Eva was still contemplating the events of the previous day, the loss of Annea and her home, but gaining a new companion. Jaryd spent his time cautiously observing for followers and trying to settle on a diplomatic approach that he could use when they arrived at Wodel. He needed to convince the town to help wage war against Abeline. This would not be an easy task.

Jaryd tried polite conversation to find out more about his new charge, but Eva terminated most of his questions with a simple yes or no, not willing to discuss herself or her feelings yet.

He reached back into his bags and pulled out a half-loaf of bread and offered it to Eva first. She broke off a piece and returned it with a simple "thank you." He then offered her his canteen which she too gratefully accepted and took a small drink. They would have to ration their food as it would be another day before reaching Wodel.

As Eva handed the water back, and Jaryd raised the lip to his mouth, it flew from his hand landing a short distance away leaking its precious contents into the sodden earth; a bolt protruding from its body.

Stunned, he looked about and saw half a dozen riders closing quickly, breath snorting from their mounts' nostrils and weapons held aloft. He cursed as they were much closer than he should have allowed. Where had they come from?

Jaryd drew his sword. "What've you got?"

"What?"

"Potions, tricks, anything?" Jaryd enquired in desperation.

Eva rummaged in her bags. She had used most of the enchantress potion already on the gatehouse guards, but her chosen alternative for use in the situation was still intact. She withdrew the bottle, larger than the previous potion, and handed it to Jaryd.

"What is it, what do I do, drink it?"

"No, no." She reached over to Jaryd and grabbed it back. "It boils water."

Jaryd looked on, confused as Eva shook the bottle,

Morning Fight

cracked it with the hilt of her sword and threw it to the ground between the advancing men and themselves.

The bottle smashed as it hit a small protruding rock and the contents didn't just dribble out, but fizzed and exploded in all directions, turning the marshy water a pale yellow colour.

Almost instantly the sodden ground began to bubble and steam, and a thin warm yellow mist started to cloak Eva and Jaryd. But the screen did not fully conceal the couple before the riders were upon them.

The riders veered off into two groups, three heading for Eva and the remainder forging a gap between her and Jaryd. Jaryd took the opportunity of the disorientating mist to strike a crippling blow to the central rider. His sword slid down the attacker's helmet and sliced into his shoulder, part severing his arm.

This was no chance attack, these riders were sent by Alvar, mercenaries under his pay and command.

Jaryd tried to edge closer to protect Eva, but the two riders engaging him could not be moved. They fought fiercely but Jaryd's control of his horse and mastery of the sword held them at bay.

He could see that Eva remained unharmed and her three assailants were either not as aggressive as the ones he had to deal with, or that they did not want to kill her. They had her surrounded and were moving her out of the dense mist that her potion had generated.

Jaryd made a fierce lunge forward unsteadying his opponents and then pulled back outmanoeuvring them to lend assistance to Eva's rear. He sidestepped one rider and rode aside Eva, pushing her back into the misty cloak.

With the additional power from his mount, they crept towards the thick screen causing her attackers to stumble and falter.

"Fly Eva. I'll hold these two." He pointed in the direction where two of her attackers were last seen. "North, deeper into the marsh. If they still follow, you'll have to swim for it."

He slapped her horse's rump and it darted off out of sight. Both of her attackers attempted to follow but Jaryd had swung down below his horse's neck and grabbed the furthest one's reins, preventing either rider from controlling their movement and following Eva.

He tussled with the panicking horses as their riders tried to pursue Eva, dodging striking blades poked aimlessly where he should've been seated.

After desperately holding on for what seemed like an eternity, providing Eva with a vital head start, his horse weakened and collapsed to its knees, rolled over and threw Jaryd into the ankle-high muddy water. His horse lay dead bleeding heavily from a long and deep slash under its neck.

He heard the sound of hooves sloshing away, but disorientated, could not determine whether they were in the same direction that Eva had taken. He lay quiet on the ground where he fell, hoping to remain hidden in the slowly clearing mist. There were no sounds around him save for the fading snorting of the riders' horses and the beat of his own heart in his chest. No movement, no shouts of command. Dare he stand?

A sharply studded gauntlet materialised out of the fog and drove forward to grip Jaryd's neck forcing any hope of standing from his thoughts. Another hand came into view wielding a short sword poised at his throat, then a helmeted face, dirty and scarred, grimaced close to him.

"Where's the pretty little girlie gone then?" he said in a rough gravely voice. The mercenary dragged Jaryd to his feet as another bound his arms behind his back.

"Let me at him, the filthy traitorous git!" Jaryd recognised the approaching man as the one he had struck during the brief fight. He was still very much alive even though his left arm now appeared quite useless. "I'm gonna chop her arms off, see how she likes it. Maybe I'll keep one as a spare."

A third mercenary came into view. "I'll slice off her face and put it on the spike on me head. Then I'll be the prettiest one round 'ere." He paraded around with a grotesque catwalk-style gait resting his hands on his hips, much to the amusement of the others who bellowed with ugly laughter.

He drew his working arm back and threw a hefty punch into Jaryd's stomach. Jaryd bent double and fell to the ground and lay on his side curled up in crippling pain.

From his position lying on the ground and with his face half covered in marsh mud, he recognized the shape of two horses through what remained of Eva's smoke screen which had now nearly cleared. Slung behind one of the riders Jaryd made out the form of a cloaked body, his heart sank.

Soul Thieves

They came to a halt in clear view of Jaryd and he tugged at the cloak and threw it to the ground. To much relief, it was in reality only her cloak.

"Girl's gone. Probably drowned in the swamp mud. Horse was just standin' there, lame and useless."

"Good meat though."

"Well, you go and get it, and sink in the mud you fat idiot."

"So, what's he worth?" Pointing at Jaryd lying on the ground.

"Not much dead or alive. Girl was though."

"Easier to get him back if he be dead."

"Good choice." The mercenary leader pulled his crossbow from his back and levelled it at Jaryd's chest. "Not getting my sword messed up over this worthless carcass."

"Wait! Save your bolt, we might need it." His immediate accomplice nodded in the direction of the forest and the path to Abeline.

Approaching slowly, was a carriage drawn by two horses with a further two attached to the rear by their reins. It was an uncommon kind of transport for these places, and indeed it was very much like ones that Alvar himself used, although he'd have a mounted escort too.

Jaryd was kicked back to the ground as he attempted to kneel while his captors waited apprehensively staring at the visitors.

"Looks like our luck's in today men. Bounty and booty."

The carriage squealed to a halt as the driver pulled his

horses to a stop and applied the brake. The mercenaries circled around, confused at the apparent deliberate action to meet with them. Usually, the sight of these robbers would mark the start of a pursuit, after which the occupants would be slain or worse, and their valuables taken. Now, however, the gold was being offered to them on a plate.

"Get out or we'll burn you out," the injured and most angry of the group barked.

"I don't think you will," came an elegant reply. The door opened and a well-dressed lady stepped out assisted by her butler, it was Ophilya.

The group of men were stunned into silence then the leader blurted, "M'lady," and bowed slightly in respect. "You're a long way from the safety of your King, you could easily be robbed." Ophilya could see that their faces were twisted with devious grins.

"My husband would have something to say about that, no doubt. I am here picking up the pieces that you seem to drop." She pointed at Eva's cloak and Jaryd lying close by. "Put him in the back."

"Oh, I don't think so, ma'am. He's worth a fair bounty, and that's what we're gonna get, back in Abeline."

"You'll get your money." Ophilya wanted to keep the upper hand for she was indeed quite vulnerable if only the mercenaries knew the truth about her.

"Er, when?"

"Now!" This was going to cost her most of what she had looted from her husband before her hasty departure.

She reached inside her jacket and removed some coins, tossing them to the leader.

"There's a lot more for the girl, now put him in the back and go and finish your task." Ophilya could be very persuasive when she sounded in command. "Hurry, I don't want to be out here all day."

Reluctantly, Jaryd was shoved into the carriage and tied to the seat. He'd finally lost all hope of protecting Eva and removing Alvar from the throne. He would have to tolerate the gloating of Ophilya and then whatever fate her husband would consider appropriate.

The horsemen remounted whilst their leader stood considering challenging Ophilya. Ophilya ignored his stance, boarded the carriage and drove slowly back in the direction of her husband's kingdom.

"They've gone m'lady," Hector called. He'd discretely looked back over his shoulder at the departing mercenaries. They didn't appear to be in too much of a hurry, but were now out of sight.

Ophilya drew a knife from her bag and bent down to cut Jaryd's bonds. The men had made a good job of securing him, and it took Ophilya quite some time to sever the ropes.

"Is that safe?" Hector's wife asked.

"Completely. Don't believe everything you hear my husband say."

Jaryd looked questioningly at the queen. He'd never been this close to her before. She was about the same age as himself, but had carried her years far better. There must be something beneficial in living in luxury he mused.

He remained on the floor of the carriage to relieve any suspicion if they were to be stopped again, but was grateful for being untied nevertheless.

"There are things you just don't know master Jaryd, and I'm surprised. When Godwyn died his soul did not pass into the hands of Varga, it passed beyond his reach and into the light, even though Varga thought that he'd barred that passage." Ophilya started to explain the situation as she saw it.

"This I have learned from the cleriks. They are not without knowledge in these matters, and remain vigilant in both worlds. Whether Alvar condemns their actions, he is powerless to prevent them. As the clerik order do not need to operate in his prized city of Abeline, they are more or less out of his reach. He doesn't treat them with any respect."

"And quite rightly so," added Jaryd. "Although the situation would appear to be less severe now, there were times when the cleriks could wield even more power than the King. I'm not sure that would ever be a good state to go back to."

Ophilya adopted a look of mild disdain towards Jaryd. Surely she was not in approval of the clerik's plots he thought.

"When Godwyn died, not only did he open the gate to enter into this paradise, he held it open long enough to send a message of guidance and knowledge back into the living world. Back into the spirit of one he loved." Did she know of this person Jaryd wondered. But for

Ophilya to know any of this, she'd have to either be in league with Varga or have deep dealings with the cleriks. Maybe, more innocently, she could be privy to Alvar's conversations with Varga. Whatever the reasons for her knowledge, Jaryd thought, Ophilya was indeed someone to be wary of.

"I will tell you this, Varga knows what Godwyn did, and he will, or already has, figured out the carrier of this wisdom. He will not stop until that person is dead and their soul rests with him.

"Alvar, my dear dim-witted husband, only believes that he can control the world by gaining the combined knowledge of you, Annea and Eva. For his loss of Eva he curses himself, and is now determined to regain her allegiance, under duress of course, control you, maybe the cleriks, and then rule forever.

"As for me, I'm sure I'll have my time in the future. But for now, I think it's time for Alvar's downfall. I'm setting you free. Our paths may meet again. Protect Eva."

So Ophilya did know.

Jaryd stood, holding the horse that Ophilya had just given him, and watched as her carriage passed out of sight in the opposite direction to Wodel. She would have to avoid Abeline and the path north beyond the marshes for some time to come.

He considered the situation for a moment. The mercenaries would be off to spend their gold. Eva was still alive, he felt it in his chest. So the only choice was made for him, ride to the east of the deep marsh, and there he'd find Eva.

To that end, this was the only part of his plans that had gone right. Walking through the marsh up to her knees was a very wet Eva, attempting to hide any trail she might leave in the mud which covered her tracks. Jaryd rode closer and then dismounted. He waded quickly to her, his heart beating with relief and excitement, and was about to embrace her.

"I thought you'd already taken a wash this morning," he said noticing her face covered in wet grass and brown mud sliding down her body. "And that perfume, it really stinks!"

"You don't look so good either." She thought about sticking her tongue out at him, but she'd probably get a mouthful of the swamp if she tried.

"I heard your horse was lame."

"A little trick I learned. Seems to work doesn't it?" Eva was leading her horse toward Jaryd, apparently, none the worse for the earlier close encounter.

They stood opposite each other, Jaryd with his face half covered in dried mud and Eva spitting grass from her mouth, and started to laugh childishly.

Prince's Home

It was a gratefully uneventful three-day ride before they arrived at the outskirts of Wodel. Certainly no scent or sound of any further mercenaries. Surely word of the failure of the previous attackers would've been relayed to Alvar by now, but perhaps he had no fear of what Jaryd could muster. Or possibly the despatched militia were not associated with the King, or gave false accounts of the events. Whatever the reason, they were relieved and rested after a night spent in decent accommodation at the inn.

Folk fell into two broad categories in the regions around Abeline. On one hand, you had those that just wanted to get on with their everyday lives. Not necessarily supporters of Alvar, but would find it far easier to betray a traveller than risk punishment for assisting them. And on the other side, there were people who were definitely resistant to Alvar, his men, and his laws. It was the latter group that Jaryd would want to gain assistance from. And it was from this company that the innkeeper belonged.

There was, of course, a much smaller third group. These were true supporters, but mercifully, their number was small.

"Jaryd, you know we're being followed?" Eva was referring to two horsemen who were keeping their distance to the south. She was unaware if Jaryd knew they were being observed. The horsemen did seem to be

Prince's Home

keeping a fair distance, and attempting to conceal themselves at every opportunity.

"Yes. Thank you. I did wonder if you had noticed them too."

Eva had the distinct impression that Jaryd was just waiting to see if she was observant enough to discover the trailers. Was Jaryd even trying to test her? She was young, her eyesight impeccable and better than most, even without the need for a seeing device, although she did keep a hand-scope in her pocket for the odd occasion where her dark brown eyes could not resolve the subject's detail.

There were few technical machines in use, and these were frowned upon in the same way as sorcerers and mystics. Plain simple people preferred the simple tools of their custom, not some fangled contraption, whether it was a small seeing aid or navigational instrument. There was no use for such items, in their opinion, simply distractions and complications to daily life.

"Eva. Dig your heels in. Let's make a little more haste."

She prodded her feet into her mount's flanks and accelerated to a gallop, Jaryd following a few lengths behind. They moved much more swiftly for a while with Jaryd taking frequent glances at the pursuers, but they were now quite a distance behind. Not deviating from their course, but also not matching Eva and Jaryd's speed.

Both obedient horses were sweating under the demand from their riders. As most trained animals would, they'd happily ride until they dropped. Jaryd knew that Wodel would be a mile clear of the next thicket, and that they would arrive well before any danger to their trusted carriers.

They careered into the light undergrowth, small branches whipping at their arms and faces. Exiting some hundred yards later into the bright morning sunlight streaming from their intended destination, they descended a gentle grassy slope and vaulted over a shallow brook and containing fence, to begin the last part of the journey up a steeper incline. At the summit, with the sun apparently higher in the sky, the small town of Wodel came into view.

Wodel was a sprawling assortment of dwellings, shops, and various businesses. It had no defined boundary as did Abeline with its walls and other various defences. With a population of less than a quarter of Abeline, many inhabitants were market traders and departed their homes to visit neighbouring towns, Abeline being the largest of the nearby ones, on a regular basis to vend their produce. It was, as the current political conditions dictated, not without sentries standing guard on the main thoroughfares into its heart.

The central part of the town was dominated by a tall steeple standing at the eastern end of the festival hall. Celebrations were notably now only conducted for marriages and harvest times. Many decades ago, social gatherings would be fairly spontaneous, with little excuse for partying.

Dotted within the few square miles that covered most

of the residences were grander two or three-storey houses. There was no slum or noble district. All citizens were considered to be equal, in stature but unlikely in wealth.

As the pair reduced speed to a kinder trot, their horses' hooves pronounced the travellers' arrival on the sandy gravel road. A sentry stirred from his stool and stood immediately to the front barring passage further into the town. He raised a gloved hand to halt the approach. He was not alone.

The weary man threw his right leg over his saddle and effortlessly dismounted. A stable boy was summoned from nearby, and took the reigns from Jaryd. He led the horse into the town and to a small stable where fresh hay and a trough would satisfy the animal's immediate needs. Eva remained on her horse as another young lad approached.

"Good morning my Lord," the sentry began the conversation. "Would you mind leaving your arms here please for the duration of your visit? I'll sign you a chitty."

"Is there a reason you'd take my blade? I'm just visiting an acquaintance."

"Rules are rules, sir. If you please," the sentry explained, and rested his own hand on the hilt of his steel.

Jaryd seized his own with his right hand and partly drew it from its scabbard.

"Hold fast!" The voice came from behind. From a recognisable cloaked figure. One of the men they'd observed following several miles back. His companion remained mounted and had a small loaded crossbow levelled at Jaryd.

Jaryd moved his palm from the sword's handle and onto the blade. He withdrew it and offered it, hilt first, back to the sentry. The sentry put forth his hands to take it but paused, then raised his gaze to meet Jaryd's eyes. There was no trickery in the sorcerer's stare, but the sentry knew this man was of importance, which of course Jaryd would always deny. Although the inscriptions on the sword were not able to be read by the sentry, he knew this was a majestic weapon, and the owner to be respected. Jaryd pushed the sword into the hesitant hands of the sentry. "I'll have that chitty if you please."

"And your companion?" Eva was already standing close to Jaryd and had removed her belt, knife and swords. She was only too happy to give these items up. They were not regular items that she'd willingly carry, but she also knew that there'd be a need to have and use them soon.

It had been a long journey, some respite would be much welcomed, except, there were urgent matters that needed attending to. "My friend, where would I find Lord Marcus?" Two cadets were beckoned and told to provide an escort to The Hall. Lord Marcus wasn't the town mayor or a town elder, but was most definitely a respected citizen. He owned and managed a couple of small holdings to the north and east, employed many people, and got deeply involved in the running of the

Prince's Home

town council. He was also distantly related to the royal line at Abeline, Godwyn being his third cousin.

The party strolled through the main road, around a small barracks, before coming to the sandstone steps of The Hall. The large double-doors were stayed open, and Jaryd was directed inside.

"We'll leave you here sir. No weapons allowed you see."

Jaryd and Eva thanked the men and walked up the stone steps. Inside, it was a grand building. Wood panelled walls, draped with tapestries and pictures, mostly depicting previous town and council elders, but some portraying the old King. But, contradictory to this perceived elegance, it wasn't lavish. The adornments were crafted by locals, not commissioned from a top-class artist. A carved stone staircase led to a first-floor balcony, from which led several closed doors, likely where the clerks would manage affairs. Jaryd had never been to Wodel before, Eva had when she was a small child, but not inside these chambers.

"Welcome to Wodel." A short plump clerk entered from a small lobby and walked behind his desk to greet the visitors. "What can I find for you, rooms, food? We have a fine local tavern just off the main square."

"In good time, thank you." Jaryd was courteous but wanted to hurry his business here. "Lord Marcus? Can you direct me to him?"

"Ah, he is in counsel with elders on the first floor. He will be finished by lunch, maybe you can return later this afternoon."

"The first floor, with the town's counsel," Jaryd repeated. "Perfect." He moved past the clerk and proceeded to climb the staircase.

"Sir, it's a private session!"

Jaryd quickened his step, followed by the heavy-breathing clerk who was overtaken by Eva's swift strides. They approached the single door, looked at one another then flung it open.

Jaryd took one step into the chamber, Eva waited on the threshold, as the clerk pushed past her to clutch Jaryd's arm.

"I know you're in mid-session, but I believe what I have to report is of great importance, to you all." Jaryd addressed the assembly with a firm voice. The clerk was still holding his arm, panting deeply.

Marcus stood and pushed his leather chair back. He looked intently at the speaker, and began to recognise him. "We've met before?" He turned his gaze past Jaryd and onto Eva who'd still not fully entered into the room. Marcus definitely remembered her face, although it has matured and rests on a woman's shoulders now.

"Many years have passed, numerous evil acts have been carried out, but yes, we've met. Abeline?"

So engrossed in the affairs of Wodel and the comfortable life he now had, Marcus had deposited his memories of his time in Abeline to the depths of his mind. He was now slowly recalling them, including ones containing the persons now standing before him. Walking around the table to confront his guests, full recollection of his knowledge of these two settled down in his thoughts. Now standing in front of Jaryd, he smiled and respectfully offered out his arms and embraced this old acquaintance.

Marcus knew that this visit must have been made under desperate circumstances, and this he would enquire into later. But now, time to renew companionships lost.

Letting go of Jaryd yet still clasping his shoulders, he identified Eva, turned his body and offered his hand. Eva raised hers to greet the tall and handsome host, and Marcus kissed it softly. He considered Eva to be an unusual companion, but there was obviously much that had or was taking place that he was not aware of. Marcus reluctantly released Eva's slender fingers and faced the other assembly members, some of which were also now standing confused.

"May I introduce Jaryd, master sorcerer of Abeline, consultant to kings, sagacious comrade, and weary traveller?" They all shared a smile and nodded greetings.

"And Eva, apprentice sorceress and companion to Annea." No denying that Marcus has correctly described her as his memory recalled, but recent events had changed her description markedly, the apprentice sorceress had recently graduated, still much to learn, but solid foundations had been provided by Annea. Eva too smiled, and greeted each one individually with positive nods.

"My Lord Marcus, as you are aware, times are not as pleasant from whence we came, and some things have to be explained now, for we need assistance." Jaryd's voice was firm but calm, and he was watching Eva as he spoke. "I think if I correct you on your description and introduction of Eva, then you will begin to realise how dire the situation is back home."

Jaryd hadn't thought about this before, but it was true, Abeline was his home, yet he really considered himself to not be attached to any one place. But as most of his time was spent there, home it was.

"Eva is no longer the apprentice to her companion Annea, for Annea is very sadly no longer with us." He looked at Eva's face and noticed her wide eyes shine with the welling tears she could not suppress. "Her recent death was the result of the evil deeds that spread within the once great kingdom. The results of the actions of the desperate Alvar."

Although saving Eva more pain from her memories of Annea and the manner of her death was very much in Jaryd's mind, he had to continue to depict the state of affairs. "Abeline has a King that dabbles with the undead, confides with Varga, and has a queen that relishes the advent of the new sciences."

"Ah, my lord Jaryd. I know of others that also dip into death. Perhaps we should shun them too." Luke spoke his mind. His was not going to be a sympathetic ear.

"Councillor, you know there lies good and evil in every community, yours too. You have an army, a small army, what's that for, rescuing pets from the drains?" Jaryd's comment raised a small laugh from Callan and Malik. But his point was not just one of humour, and hopefully, it wouldn't be taken as such.

Callan was a stately elder. He had come to Wodel at the time of Alvar's crowning. Given no real choice, as Godwyn's close friend and chief of staff, disappear or die at the new King's hand were his two options. But had his loyalty to the old King and kingdom waned, or could he still muster enthusiasm for revenge?

The old farmer Malik was tired of managing his fields. Duties that he would have wanted his two sons to adopt, but they were lost in battle fighting alongside Godwyn's forces, against Alvar.

Marcus interrupted the conversations that were obviously heading the wrong way. "Please, be seated. No point warring within this council too."

The three men and woman of the council returned to their seats, with Marcus sitting in between the four. Opposite Marcus sat Jaryd with Eva taking a small stool just behind him. The clerk sat down at a small desk and dutifully began minuting the conversations.

No thought was given to their missed lunch, one of the main motivations to actually attend these dreary gatherings, while they heatedly discussed the options that Jaryd was detailing to them. The suggestion to raise armies against Alvar was put to a vote. Callan and Malik gave positive responses, but Luke and Shorna counteracted these. Marcus, with the deciding vote, declined to make a choice. Progress, from Jaryd's viewpoint, was slow if indeed non-existent, he was tired of the last few days, and of the last few hours' discussions and debating. He stood with his head held less high than usual, dejected.

"Let's eat!" Malik followed Jaryd and Eva towards the exit. The other councillors stood and followed. "Some good food and relaxation will be a remedy for you."

The party left the room with Marcus at the head and the clerk bringing up the rear after securing the door.

"Jaryd, we'll talk more after lunch. But let's just relax a little now." Marcus was trying to be as reassuring as possible, and suggesting the situation may change.

A glint of light from Jaryd's left alerted him to movement on the balcony. Light from a prohibited dagger in the belt of a man he recognised as an attacker just three days ago. The dagger remained at the man's side, but in the crook of his left arm was rested a short cross-bow, loaded with a steel bolt. The aim was towards Marcus. The invader squeezed the trigger and the bolt flew. It flashed fast, straight and true. Jaryd was just one step behind Marcus, but was unable to react with enough haste to prevent the bolt from striking home.

A small brown-cloaked figure rushed and jumped past the procession on the staircase, in front of Jaryd, and in front of Marcus. They heard a dull thud and then the clerk fell onto the floor with limbs sprawled out. Sentries had appeared on the balcony from doors leading to spiral stairs. The assassin dropped his unloaded weapon and fled through a narrow door, closely pursued by two guards.

Marcus reached the downed man and rolled him onto his side. The head of the bolt was completely embedded in his side, and he was bleeding steadily from the corner of his mouth, blood dripping onto the floor marking the spot where he'd sacrificed himself.

Jaryd could tell that the body was lifeless. "Does that convince you of the need for a rebellion?" It was a callous remark, out of character, but did achieve the desired effect on Marcus.

Marcus stood, laying down the limp body to rest. He looked past Jaryd and into the frightened and angry eyes of the four councillors. "Gather your brave men, arm and train them. We go to fight!"

Alvar and the Devil

The dungeons in Abeline were overflowing with captives. People from all over the city, young and old, women and children, the poor and wealthy, were being rounded up and detained for questioning. Questioning in the method of Alvar, by some of his most sadistic followers. Cruel men of lesser caring than beasts and animals, and with even lesser morality.

Confessions to all sorts of crimes were easy to obtain, but none were genuine. A tortured limb or extracted tooth could even provide testament that black was white. Alvar knew no other means by which to discover accurate information, and was frustrated by the results he was now achieving.

He was brought up in the shadow of his brother's achievements, always coming second. He was the one that fought in battle, for the benefit of his father's lands. He was the one that led armies of hapless soldiers, yet still realised victories in the face of adversity. He was the son that defended his kingdom and put his life in jeopardy. Yet his brother, Godwyn, was protected within castle walls. It was Godwyn, the eldest, that was fated to become the king.

In Alvar's mind, it was all totally unjust. Godwyn was nothing, but by his birthright, the eldest son, was to become the king. He had hated the situation every minute of every day that Godwyn was still alive. He knew he would be the great leader and vowed, on the crowning of his brother, that he would take what should rightfully be his.

Since the disappearance of Eva and Jaryd, Alvar had not begun to calm down. Someone had to have some information about their whereabouts. Rewards were being offered, obscene amounts of money. Titles and land were presented to owners with information that would lead to the recapture of, what Alvar described as, traitors to the crown. Regardless of what was on offer, not a single peasant, farmer, or banker came forward to claim their new lifestyle.

He had instructed his seers to delve into the absolute lowest depths of their psyche to unearth his prey. Many men and women professed to have inhuman powers, most were simply gipsies, some were deranged and ought to have been locked out of sight, but none had the ability to perform the required tasks. Possibly only two people could. Unfortunately, one, Annea, lay dead in the mortuary, and the other was one of the people he was trying to ensnare.

And what of his mercenaries that he had sent to all points of the compass? What had transpired from that scheme, nothing! Had they just taken his money and run, were they looking in the wrong direction, had they been defeated themselves?

Annoyed, irritated and totally at his wits end, Alvar stormed from the upper ramparts outside his bedroom, and into his receiving hall. An old man stood before him clutching his ragged hat and cradling a short walking staff. His head was bowed and his lips were trembling.

"Speak!"

"Your majesty. I, I have two sons. They are in your dungeons."

"And do they have information? What can they tell me?"

"I'm sure they no nothing, sire."

"Do you have information for me?" this was starting to become tiresome for Alvar.

"Your majesty, please. Let my sons go," the old man pleaded. "I was once a seer, I could make an effort to be again."

"Ah, right. I'm not an unreasonable man. I let your precious offspring out to act out more treacherous deeds, and you try and see for me?"

"Yes sire, I will try." The man stepped closer holding out his crumpled hat in his hands, looking straight into Alvar's dark eyes.

"How about, I keep your sons locked up, and lock you up too!" Alvar's tone had changed from a quiet diplomatic voice to a beastly roar. "Ten minutes. See for ten minutes. I hope you can recall your long-lost talents."

The old man sat down cross-legged and laid his staff in front, pointing towards Alvar, then folded his arms. He began to sway and mutter unintelligible chants. There was a rhythm to his prayers which encroached into the mind, threatening to pull memories out and available for others to see. This man was a seer, or had been a long time ago.

Alvar paced around the room, the chanting got more intense, and the guards started to become agitated. The seer was stumbling about inside the thoughts of everyone in the room. Ten minutes elapsed. Then fifteen. The chanting slowed, and came to a stop. An air of relaxation descended upon those present.

"Well, old man. Did you see outside of this room?" Even Alvar had the ability to probe the undefended mind of somebody close when he put his heart into it.

"Sorry, no." Tears formed in his eyes. He had failed in the presence of the King, and knew his future.

Alvar leaned close to his face so he could easily smell the fear in his sweat. "Pathetic!" He stood up straight, looked down at the helpless aged man, turned his back and walked away. "To the cells. Take him to the cells!"

Two guards drew up and secured a firm grip under his arms, pulling him along the floor towards the door like an old mop.

"Have mercy on my sons!"

Another complete waste of time.

Alvar dismissed his guards and closed the doors. He was now in such a desperate condition, devoid of real information outside of his realm, lost in thoughts like a stranded sailor at sea, with not a hint of a breeze to get him home.

"Well, I've done it before," he mumbled to himself. "I'll be prepared. It'll be perfectly safe."

He slipped into his study, avoiding the blood-stained floor where his wife had brought about the death of a friend, and returned with several of the remaining articles from his collection. He stood in the doorway and placed the items on the floor and on small tables all around himself, and all within easy reach if the need arose. The stone floor under the doorway would be the thickest point in this room, and it'd be far easier to breach the walls or floor elsewhere.

Varga was meandering through his dominion, lifting up the occasional drifting soul to see if they were of use or if any satisfaction could be gained by taunting it, when he felt a strange but familiar tug at his own essence. It was scarcely a summons, nobody had ever achieved that or would be stupid enough to try, however, he did sense a call to depart from here and travel into the land of the living. An oddly compelling desire to follow the calling voices in his head, he decided to submit to the temptation, and make the swift journey into life.

He emerged, as Alvar had predicted, a few yards from where he stood. Not in front of him, but behind in his store, next to the remnants of his collection. The attraction to the contents was obviously alluring, certainly more so than the other empty rooms. He sniffed the containers, and he appeared to recognise some of the beings within. Beings that should ordinarily be in his own kingdom, not entrapped here.

He turned to observe the rest of the room and noticed the dark patch of recent death in the corner. This brought some excitement into his presence. Then he sharply raised his gaze onto Alvar, whose breathing had become shallow, partly in fear and partly as not to make too much sound.

Alvar and the Devil

Whereas Alvar would play with the souls of the dead, Varga reciprocated and would entertain himself with the spirits of living humans, torn from the real world and transported into his own. With his knowledge of the human form, and from his own personal collection of fresh spirits, he could assume a rather good approximation to a living person. Perhaps a bit grey at the edges, but sufficient for him to endure this place.

"Ah, I thought it might be you." Varga, having created a human-like form far taller than even the most dominating man, looked down at Alvar. "Are we having some trouble? I assume that is why you are feeling the need to converse with your superior."

Alvar was somewhat flustered by the physical appearance of Varga, but he controlled his discomfort and stared directly at Varga's bold attempt at a human face. Two eyes, a nose, and a good attempt at a mouth, but there was something not quite right about having teeth but no lips. "You may well be the sovereign in your underworld empire, but in the land of the living, my lands, you will not frighten me."

They both took a moment to assess the situation and compose themselves for the next flurry of exchanges. Varga moved slightly away from Alvar's shelves. Although encouraged by what he felt in some containers, he was slightly alarmed at some bottles where he could not see the contents, but assumed that they could transpire to be a hazard.

Alvar was first to resume the conversation. "To come straight to the point, I need a little assistance." He didn't want to show his whole hand at such an early stage of negotiations, but he was also not in a mind to dawdle either. At least Alvar hadn't said he was desperate for help, but he had laid himself open to attack.

"So, there is something in your little life that needs an otherworld's help? Can this really be true, Alvar the magnificent asking for help?" Varga attempted a lip-less smile which looked more like that of a greeting from a strange and angry dog.

Alvar was determined not to be distracted by inconsequential verbal banter, and carried on with his upfront questioning. "You can see far and deep, and that is all that I ask of you now. I assume you have not misplaced any of your capabilities during your summons here." He was playing a risky hand. To consider himself the master of Varga, and that he was in control of Varga's existence here could earn himself a swift death.

"So, you've played your cards. You need my help but still, try and belittle me. Presupposing you don't actually want me to return to my non-summonsed space, what do you want?"

Alvar had to be blunt, lest he wished to lose what could be his last hope to see what need be done. "Where is Jaryd, where is that little girl Eva, and what plans are they preparing to execute?"

Varga was still, and quiet. Alvar sensed that his mind was elsewhere, seeing other places. His shape started to dissolve slowly around the main features, especially the face. Then his existence was resumed and he had an even bigger grin on his face.

Alvar and the Devil

"As you've been so totally plain with me, I can tell you what you want to know. But, what do you offer in return?"

"I can offer you souls of dead men, or women, children even."

"Those I can get easily enough already. What do you think occupies my time? Do you think I have so few souls to arrange that I can spend all day playing games?" Varga wanted more, something that he would eventually get, but he was becoming impatient too.

Alvar too knew that to gain the upper hand in this life, he would have to sacrifice something dear now.

"My soul!"

Varga remained completely calm externally. Within, he was doing cartwheels with joy. "Agreed. You willingly and without condition, give your soul to me, and I will see your answers."

"No! Not without condition. Won't I die without my soul?"

"Don't fret my worried small friend." Compared to Varga's current form, most men in the kingdom would appear short. "I will take care of your prized spirit. Only when a spirit passes to its final resting place, outside of my domain, will the human form completely die, and we don't want that do we."

"I agree. You will have my soul, you will take it into safekeeping, and I will possess it again later." This was much to ask, but Alvar could always negotiate from this position and settle on something less. "And, you will assist me as necessary until my kingdom is secure."

As much as Varga desired to take Alvar's soul, this was much to agree to, especially since the prize would be his eventually in any case.

"Final deal. Your soul, my assistance for one year, or 'til death do you part."

Varga knew he had the upper hand. Alvar knew the great advantage he would receive. The contract was settled.

Varga hesitated not even until the ink on the imagined bond was dry. It was an unremarkable event. Alvar's soul left him and travelled quickly into the body of Varga. None of the lingering wispy departures that were more usual when a soul departed a living body. Alvar's body made a single shudder, and it was over.

The King stood feeling absolutely normal, physically. Within his mind, so many burdens appeared to have been removed. What little regard he had for his subjects vanished. His desires for physical pleasures waned. But his hunger to live in complete control enlarged.

"Tell me Jaryd's plans, where is Eva, what should I do?"

"Firstly, my soul-less friend, Eva is no little girl. She has grown up much recently. Forced to by your own hand. She needs close watching.

"Jaryd does not seem to be a threat to you. He is a wise and tricky character indeed, but he will not wield his sword and slay you.

"They are both in Wodel, and securing forces for a rebellion.

"Finally, for today, you need to resurrect your armies.

"No more questions now. You can request further conferences later."

Now Alvar knew what he couldn't discover using his usual methods, mercenaries, scouts, informers. But at the highest price bar death itself. "What have I done?" He mulled this information over in his mind and then snapped back to reality. Varga had disappeared.

A rapid knock sounded on the door leading to the main upper hallway, followed by an armed guard and an out-of-breath young boy bursting through. The boy was red in his face and beads of sweat were formed on his forehead, coming together and running down his cheek. The messenger carried a small leather bag on a strap over his shoulder.

"Your majesty," he spoke softly between deep breaths. "I have ridden hard for two nights and a day from the wooded outskirts of Wodel in the east. I bare a note from your frontline scouts." He handed it straight to Alvar and bowed low.

Alvar opened the shoulder bag and hesitantly removed a single piece of folded paper. On it, scratched with dried blood, was simply written *A storm is brewing, prepare yourself. Let your soul bring victory.*

Gathering an Army

After the events at the council chambers, Marcus walked with the travelling couple to his home a few streets from the offices. Although regarded as the town's leader, and maybe even King, his residence is not of a grand palace as is Alvar's, but a more informal and restrained home.

As the three walked the two shallow steps to his front door, it was opened by his wife Tiana. She stood a little taller than her husband, and elegantly displayed her stature as the town elder's spouse.

She had shoulder-length straight hair and bore a few scars on her face acquired during battles some distance in the past judging by the faintness of their form. Her hands though, were smooth and soft and did not portray the owner as a fighting woman.

It was evident that the couple were from different backgrounds, a warrior and a diplomat.

Tiana greeted her husband at the threshold with a firm kiss and embrace. She'd never had the pleasure of making Jaryd's acquaintance, but as he was introduced, she became fully aware of who he was. The infamous physician of Abeline, and reclusive sorcerer. Jaryd and Tiana exchanged courteous bows.

Tiana turned to Eva with a questioning expression waiting for her husband's introduction. "This is Eva, Annea's long-time companion and student, who has so recently departed."

Tiana's expression mirrored Eva's sorrowful appearance, for she had become instantly aware of Eva's love for Annea and her great loss. Perhaps Tiana was deeper than a brave warrior, perhaps she could see emotions before they had revealed themselves to others in her company.

Eva was unsure of whether to bow, curtsey or shake her hand. She settled on a stumbling curtsey-bow and bent her head low. Her medallion swung forward and glinted in the late afternoon sunshine, attracting Tiana's attention. As she straightened up, she held the medallion and secured it within her shirt.

"My dear." Tiana recognised the jewel and wondered about its origin. "That's very pretty. You don't see that quality often."

"It was a gift from Annea. I think it's a locket, but it does not open."

The front of the locket, with its pentagonal decoration, was a familiar design from many decades past. Such motifs fell from fashion coincident with Godwyn's removal from the throne, but Tiana was familiar with the style. It was a royal locket that typically only adorned the necks of royalty and their most trusted friends. This was something which she assumed Eva was unaware of, and Tiana did not want to delve deeper into its history yet.

"Come, Eva. Let's get you inside and rested." Tiana put her arm around Eva's back and onto her shoulder then led her into her home.

Jaryd watched Eva as she entered the house and realised just what a delicate creature Eva was. Not only had she lost the closest person to a mother that she'd ever known, but she'd now be more inquisitive about Tiana's interest in her medallion. He felt a paternal-like urge to protect her from any further hurt, and followed closely behind.

Marcus and Jaryd sat in deep chairs around a recently lit fire. The nights were drawing in and there was a chill in the air. The harvests would have to be made before the early winter frosts arrived. But, even though Jaryd knew the importance of the harvest, he felt uneasy about permitting so many able-bodied workers to tend the fields when they should be aiding in his proposed rebellion against Alvar.

They sipped slowly from two large tumblers of a delicious brandy-wine, and smelled appealing aromas emanating from the kitchen where Tiana and Eva were helping to prepare dinner. No doubt Eva was assisting with some unique spicing, to rejuvenate both mind and body.

Thoroughly relaxed and warmed by his drink, Jaryd was not distracted from pursuing his quest. "So, when do we start to plot against your neighbour the King?" He wanted revenge and retaliation on behalf of Annea, the people of Abeline, and most of all, Eva.

"Tonight. We should have guests arriving shortly. We'll discuss our opportunities then." Marcus had just as much reason to want Alvar taken care of. He had spent much of his youth in the castle at Abeline, so knew only too well the tricks and deeds that Alvar was capable of. Marcus's father was Godwyn's wife's brother. Not blood-related, but too closely related for Marcus to speak about. He fled Abeline with his parents but, like Eva, he too lost a loved one during his escape. Maybe the time was right for old scores to be settled.

It was a sombre evening after the death of the council's clerk. There was no jollity in the air even though drink was freely offered. There was grave business to attend to.

Callan arrived first, knocking with determined intent. Tiana greeted him before he had time to break his cane on the door. He entered into Marcus's and Jaryd's discussions about the removal of Alvar, or more accurately, the attempt to remove him.

Luke and Malik arrived together shortly afterwards, followed, lastly, by Shorna. All four guests, Marcus and Jaryd, moved into the dining room and were seated around a traditional low Wodel table. A table of friendship, unlike the grandiose affair in Alvar's palace. Marcus's table was simply decorated, with a bowl of fruit and some candles. But what was missing in terms of splendour was easily compensated for by the excellent company.

Jaryd had posed them all a question about what Alvar would do next. Not about a rebellion, but his actions to further deepen his control over his people and those close neighbours. Excited debates flooded around the table when Marcus realised that the hectic sounds from the kitchen were noticeably absent. He interrupted the conversation as he raised his hand. There were still two important guests missing from the room.

The door to the hallway opened quietly and there stood Tiana, the woman of Marcus's heart, and Eva, a woman who would melt any man's heart. Tiana was wearing her finest dress and jacket, they had seen better days, but still portrayed her in all her splendour. Eva stood beside her, a good bit shorter and more petite, wearing a borrowed white belted dress that draped over the floor like a bride on her wedding day. Tiana led her to a seat furthest from the doorway lest the draught chilled her open back.

Jaryd was conscious that his eyes lingered far too long on Eva, but he was not alone and nobody else would've noticed.

Eva had never owned such magnificent robes or dressed so feminine, and was transported away from these testing times to a childhood dream as a fairytale princess. She was aware, but not embarrassed, of the other guests' attention, and directed her own gaze to Jaryd with a girlish grin spread wide across her mouth.

A simple but truly delicious meal was served and all ate heartily, leaving nothing except fish-bones and the plates they rested upon.

The night was getting late and the table had been cleared. Marcus had supplied paper and quills for anyone that wanted to make notes and plans of their actions.

Gathering an Army

"Can we first see who is in favour of any form of action here," Marcus asked.

"You can count me in," Callan immediately replied. "But you ask a difficult question. I can only speak for myself, I do not have an army, but simple labourers."

"But these issues do affect all," Jaryd added. "Most men in your villages and towns have fought before, will they fight once again?"

"I believe so," said Callan. "I will not force any to take up arms, but I expect to gather the majority of able-bodied men, and some women to support us too."

Both Marcus and Jaryd's hopes were uplifted on hearing Callan's decision. But the remaining members would be harder to ally.

Malik got to his feet and clasped Marcus's hand between his own. "For all of those lost in battle, I'm with you both and Callan too."

Marcus had expected nothing less from Callan and Malik, but he knew Luke would be challenging and Shorna even more so.

A short period when nobody spoke passed, and then Luke, as all but Shorna's eyes were upon him, stood.

"I am old and cannot enter into battle again. Whilst my thoughts are with all you that undertake this mission, it must be without me." Luke looked solemnly around the table. "I would wish that my people would join you, but a leader from my town would be from a younger generation. And they do not fully understand the necessity of the task."

"We need your men. It will only be by weight of

numbers, of swordsmen, archers and horsemen that we stand any chance of success." Jaryd was more forceful in his request. "I beg you to find your most courageous captain, and join us in this struggle."

Luke retook his seat and turned to Shorna hoping to guide the meeting in her direction. Shorna was inclined back in her chair with her hands resting on her lap. Of all those seated around her, she was most concerned at Jaryd's reaction to what she would say. Her town was far further east than the others, and Alvar's taxmen were too lazy to venture there that frequently.

"I…" she hesitated as she gathered courage, then continued. "I'm sorry. I understand your plight, but it is too great a risk. My people live in peace. We will help in any other way, but I cannot put their lives in danger."

Marcus understood her decision and held Jaryd's arm to prevent him from standing to argue. "We will be indebted to you for anything you can provide, horses, food, weapons, anything."

Eva had long since returned from her brief fairy-tale dream, and was now firmly seated in reality, where each decision that was made would inevitably cost the lives of citizens during battle; lives of men who would leave grieving families behind. She appreciated the consequence of war, the loss of life, and the principles that drove such encounters. For the sadness that conflicts brought, and for the bravery of those here now, she shed a small tear, but there was nothing that she sought to add to the debate regardless of her feelings about Alvar.

Gathering an Army

As the four visitors prepared to leave, Marcus insisted that Jaryd and Eva would be their guests for tonight. For this kind offer, they were truly thankful.

As the group approached the front door, shouting and screams were heard from outside. Luke opened the door to the sight of fearful men and women running to fetch pails of water to extinguish a blaze that was engulfing the top floor of the town hall.

Marcus grabbed a passerby. "What happened?"

"Four men on horses rode through and began attacking anyone caught on the street, then they threw burning torches in through the windows."

"What men? Did you recognise them?" Luke asked as he stepped forward to question the man.

Fearfully the man replied, "They looked like men, but wore grey ragged robes and their faces were like death. Someone said they were risen again dead controlled by King Alvar."

"Do not fear such stories. These are just men dressed to scare and frighten you. Alvar's men no doubt." Jaryd paused. "Nobody controls the dead."

He tried to pacify the panicked citizens. He knew that his statement was not the complete truth, but surely Alvar had not the power over the dead. He was a minor magician, not a necromancer.

The fire was under control and it didn't appear to have caused significant damage. Two men had received blows to their heads during the attack, but they were only mildly concussed. From Jaryd's point of view, all he noticed were the actions of a desperate man attempting to terrorise these people into submission. However, for Alvar to attack people in Wodel would mean that he most likely knew that he and Eva were here.

Jaryd turned to Marcus for a private conversation. "I believe Alvar knows I am here and this is designed to suppress your rebellion, showing you a little of his strength by the control of these false dead men. These attacks will continue until your strength of will is beaten down, or will force you to attack him in anger and in an unprepared state. He will bait you or bludgeon you, but only if we stay here. Our presence is placing you in danger, and we must leave tomorrow."

"You will remain as my guests, as our town's guests. We will gather our soldiers and march on Abeline in two days." Marcus was defiant, and looked as if he had taken Alvar's bait. "He may have a larger number of men at his disposal to command, but we have experienced tacticians and hope in our stomachs, and this hope will fuel our defeat of his regime."

"I will put my trust in your hope, but will rely on my sword to defeat this tyrant." Jaryd had succeeded in starting to build his army.

Attack on Alvar

Over the next two days, the sun rose, set and went down. Nothing unusual occurred. No attacks by Alvar's men or mercenaries, and no evidence of his scouts.

The regular bustle of the town had changed. Gone was the everyday trading that normally took place in the markets and shops, and replaced by an increase in the activities at the blacksmith's and carpenter's workshops. The construction of pots and pans and furniture had been replaced with that of armour, swords and bows.

Tents, marquees and other temporary accommodations were being erected to the south of the town, close to the town's outskirts but far enough away to reduce congestion as men, women, and eldest children arrived to perform their obligations. As was promised by the council meeting at Marcus's home, nobody had been forced to travel to Wodel. All attendance was voluntary and out of respect for their masters, even though the risk of fatality on the battlefield was high.

The council members had also arrived, with the exception of Shorna who had previously voiced her concerns about the safety of her people.

Each of the leaders was already wearing their battledress, armour and cloaks decorated with respective coats of arms, with swords at their side.

Jaryd and Eva were being fitted with light armour too. Along with the generals, they'd fight alongside Marcus and his allies. The light armour, consisting of a thin but strong metal chest-plate and a leather vest, would provide some protection during the skirmishes to come, but were trivial in comparison to what Alvar's elite would bear. They'd be clad in mail and full-body heavy armour. Mounted, these men would make an alarming and formidable foe, but the weight would be a disadvantage, and that was the faith of Wodel's war planners.

The continuous deployment and return of Marcus's scouts had provided useful information. Alvar did not appear to have started setting out his armies in preparation for battle. Indeed, the only apparent indication that he was even in preparation was the increase in guards at the city limits, and that all stall-holders had now retreated to within the castle walls. But he was no fool. As he brought all of the outlying provisions, food stalls, and livestock, within his walls' protection, he would be in a position to defend a siege for many weeks, if not months.

Breaching the castle walls in a siege situation would be nigh-on impossible for Marcus to achieve. The defended castle wall of Abeline had just one main gate. Minor gates would be sealed by stone walls moved into place, leaving the heavy portcullis as the major obstacle. But this would be protected and shielded by archers atop the parapets. Given enough time, Marcus could launch attack after attack on the gate, but with his limited fighting force, he would soon be weakened by losses inflicted by burning oil and arrows, leaving himself a target for an offensive attack by Alvar.

"Jaryd," Marcus asked, "our generals have

considered the options available for this battle. They feel they have but a single choice, to construct wooden platforms to bring against the lesser defended walls, east and west, and to invade directly pushing our men over the walls and into the castle."

"Under any normal situation, that is a suitable plan. However, do they propose to cut down the trees forming our own defences in order to build these structures? And when we're building and positioning them, will we be open to attack?"

"My Lord Jaryd," Karel, Marcus's most loyal friend and experienced general, had been listening to their discussion on the attack plans. "I have used this technique before, and it works well. We will build defences to restrict the opposition's movement outside their own gates."

"That'll take too long, and I know of the occasions where you've used this before. They were upon strong walls but few men behind them. Here, we don't know the number in Alvar's squad, but we must expect them to be plentiful." Jaryd could not see this plan succeeding. The allied army would grow restless and even depart to return to their homes if the blockade became drawn out.

Karel was becoming annoyed at Jaryd for discarding his strategy so quickly. "So, from your years of experience in combat, what would you propose?"

"I submit most gracefully to your superior knowledge of military tactics, but I have the advantage of knowing what you do not. We attack the main gate, the portcullis."

What appeared to be the most ridiculous suggestion

that Karel had ever heard, brought him to the point where his anger could not be contained. "Marcus, my friend, if you follow this madman I will retreat with my company." He turned his back on Jaryd and faced Marcus for a reply.

"Tonight, after the business of this town has subsided, and if, as I'm sure she will, Eva has worked accurately today, I will show you my plan." Eva had not accompanied Jaryd that day, but had taken some help to scour the town for a few selected components for a special recipe. And this recipe would provide the dessert after supper.

Night had fallen and an eerie quietness befell the town and outlying grounds. After the activity during the day preparing for the forthcoming conflict, the soldiers, their attendants and families, and the majority of the public had retired for necessary slumber.

Marcus and Karel were waiting a short distance from the encampments near the small wooded region just out of sight of the guards patrolling the area. Their breath steamed in the cold autumn air as they pulled tight their coats to keep in their bodies' warmth. They stood silently awaiting Jaryd's arrival.

Then, gradually, a warm lamp light grew brighter as it swayed closer, illuminating Jaryd and his accomplice Eva. Jaryd carried a long bar whilst Eva cradled a small wooden casket in both arms close to her chest. They walked down the grassy bank to join the waiting pair out of sight of any potential onlookers or spies.

Attack on Alvar

"Thank you for taking the time to allow us to perform a small demonstration." Jaryd didn't dither, set the lantern on the ground and raised the iron bar above his head with both arms. When at full stretch, he plunged one end firmly into the earth where it remained planted firmly upright.

Eva stepped forward into the bathing yellow glow, knelt at the base of the bar and placed the casket down, pushing it close to the metal. She opened the lid to reveal a fine black sparkling powder. Just a small amount, perhaps only a few handfuls.

Karel gave a small snort. "I've seen black flash powder before. It may knock a few heavy men from their feet when lit, but you'll need a cartload to bend the bars on the castle's gate."

Jaryd raised a gloved finger to his eye and then pointed at the open casket. From his pocket, he removed a long taper, lit it in the lantern flame and persuaded the others to step back to a safe distance. Jaryd, standing with the watching party, flicked the taper into the box.

The glowing end rested on the surface of the powder, but there was no flash. After several seconds, the glow of the taper was overshadowed by the illumination that was emanating from the shimmering surface of the box's contents. A few sparks spat forth in the direction of the pole. Then a steady stream of flashing specks flowed like a red river towards the pole and rose upwards until it was entirely engulfed. It stood for a minute with shimmering and swirling red and black patterning covering the iron, and then the glow descended back to the ground, all of

Soul Thieves

the powder having been consumed. A few isolated sparks randomly scurried across the earth, and then all was still.

The remaining strands of smoke drifted away in the light breeze to allow the onlookers a chance to see the outcome. The iron bar was gone. In its place lay a rounded mass that was once the pole.

"We'll need to manufacture a small sackful which will take one or two days, with help. Placed by the gate, it will burn our entrance into the castle grounds." Jaryd was outlining his earlier plan. "It cannot be dowsed by water, and any interfering prodding by the gate's guards will result in their weapons burning too."

Eva stood and smiled as Jaryd pointed out her achievement. "We have all the ingredients, but need you to provide us some assistance." After her earlier reluctance to speak at the meetings, she now spoke assertively to Marcus.

"I compliment you on your entertainment," Karel spoke dismissively. "But we still have to place this powder by the gate. Surely a suicidal mission should anyone even accept."

Eva did not know Jaryd's complete plan, she had only the one assignment to perform, and her smile slowly sank from her face at Karel's words.

"Polish your shields. Bright enough to shave with. Then we'll announce our intent to Alvar at sun-up in three days' time. I trust you will be ready?"

"To die!" Karel sneered.

"To win!" Jaryd added.

Attack on Alvar

From just within the outskirts of a small forest a little less than a mile from the walls of Abeline castle, Marcus, Karel, and Jaryd were standing and staring through the light covering of trees and morning haze towards the castle's side wall. The mist settled knee-deep and dense on the ground, and flowed from the river to the north, across the gated wall, past the readying troops and on into the forest behind them.

"Sun-up in less than an hour. Gather your men and take your positions." Karel indicated the first stage of the attack was to begin. Marcus had gladly put Karel's experience to good use and he was effectively directing the sequence of attacks.

"Callan, Marcus. Proceed to the south side of the castle. Keep your distance from their archers and face them with your backs to the sunrise." It was late autumn and the sun didn't rise too high in the sky, appearing from the south-east.

Callan and Marcus commanded over three hundred armed archers, swordsmen, and fighters wielding any sort of implement that they could find. A dozen men were mounted and led the march into position, banners unfurled atop lengthy pikes.

Karel himself took the majority of the remaining force and slowly edged forward on the western wall. Again, out of range of Alvar's bowmen, he raised his hand and the advancing army halted behind him.

Malik guided the small company to the north gated wall. He was accompanied by Jaryd, Eva and Tiana, with Eva's saddlebags full with its contents waiting to dispatch a message to Alvar.

"Missy." Malik was an elder who'd lived his life in the traditional manner, women would not be involved in men's work such as this. "A woman's place is at home or tending the injured, not here in the frontline."

"Sadly I have no home, fortunately, there are no injured, so I guess I'll stay here with you." Eva ignored Malik's stares and trotted calmly toward Jaryd to her right, who had a restrained grin spreading on his face.

Malik's army was not the tough fighting force that the other two regiments comprised, but were nonetheless some of the most important on the battlefield. They wore their town's colours on their tunics over metal breastplates, and each carried a leather-over-metal shield in one hand, and various bludgeoning weapons in the other.

Jaryd had been observing the castle's defendants with his hand-scope at frequent intervals during their march to the front of the castle. "There seems to be an even spread of soldiers around the battlements, perhaps less on the south side, and I suspect few on the east where they have no direct opposition from us."

All were now in position and the anticipated attack waited for the first rays of sunlight over the shoulders of Marcus and his followers. As the sun rose, its rays of light shone down onto Alvar's men silhouetting his defending army as the attackers started their approach. In the centre of the assault was a wall-high wooden tower being driven forwards on four wheels powered by heavy oxen like giant hamsters in wheels.

Attack on Alvar

A volley of arrows flew from the battlements and into Marcus's attacking army. A warning was shouted and the troops halted. Bending to their knees with shields above them, the arrows impaled into the hard wood or leather, or missed completely in the large gaps between the spread-out group. The arrows were retrieved and passed to Marcus's archers who returned fire but not reaching the height of the wall. The first exchange in battle was over and Marcus advanced further.

He could advance and defend in this method until he was just out of range of the crossbows. A bolt would fly through a defender's shield unlike the arrows used for long-range shots. But it was not his plan to jeopardise the safety of his men.

He came to a standstill with only a couple of men injured by the onslaught of arrows, and signalled for the tower to forge on. High on the ramparts Alvar had commanded an increase in his men, and this movement was visible by Marcus's scouts. The scout lowered his banner. On the west side, Karel responded and lowered his too.

Jaryd, on the north side, was still in the castle's shade, but he had also noticed the thinning of cover above the gate as Abeline's soldiers were repositioned to the south wall. It would soon be time, he could see behind him the treetops illuminated by the morning sun.

Karel watched and waited, taking no direct part, but ready to reinforce either the north or south as required.

A slow apprehensive fifteen minutes passed until the sun was touching the tops of the heads of the crouching men in Malik's squad. Malik gave his command and the squad removed their tunics revealing their shining armour. On his second command, the soldiers stood upright into the full glare of the mid-morning sun and turned their shields leather side to face their bodies, revealing the gleaming finish on the inside facing their enemy on the battlements atop the castle walls.

The dazzling sun's rays reflected from the mirrored surfaces of the armour and shields and bounced back into the eyes of their opponents, dazzling their vision which had been upon dark shadows just seconds earlier.

"Loose!" Malik's final command of the operation sounded out and a flight of arrows flew from the bows of the advancing archers. They were within range of Alvar's bowmen but they could not target the allies through the blinding beams of sunlight. Malik's archers advanced yet further and let another barrage of shots fly to their target seeking the bodies of the light-stricken castle occupants.

Eva stood next to Malik with her horse's reins held firmly. Malik turned to Eva and took them from her grasp.

"This is my task. Don't argue and stand back." Eva tried to grip onto the reins but Malik's pull was too hard. "I'll see you in our castle later."

For an elder, he mounted the horse with ease and swiftness, and galloped to the gate, with Eva's saddlebags of powder bouncing on the horse's flanks. It was a short ride from where Eva remained behind the attacking archers, to the portcullis, and Malik had already come to a stop to dismount and secure the packages in place.

After his rapid dismount, he reached behind the saddle and released one bag, catching it and seizing it under his left arm. An opportune shot from one of Alvar's gate defenders glanced off of the horse's shoulder causing him to rear up dislodging the remaining sack of powder.

Malik reached down lifting the second package under his other arm, and ran the few remaining strides to the gate, throwing the bags down roughly into the correct position. He unsheathed his sword and thrust it between the bars striking the enemy before he had the opportunity to reload. It struck home deep into his groin and he doubled over in pain releasing a muffled whimper as he fell.

Malik fell to his knees and pushed the two sacks firmly under the lower bar of the portcullis and reached into his pocket to retrieve his flint and tinder. With these in his hand, he was just about to complete the task when two pike-men lunged forward sinking both points into Malik's chest. The flint fell to the ground and Malik staggered and fell dead but suspended on the pikes which remained in his body.

Eva let out an enraged scream and ran forward to ignite her powder sacks. As she ran past Jaryd he stretched out an arm and grabbed her around the waist pulling her close and inhibiting her from receiving a similar fate to Malik. She pounded at Jaryd's chest and yanked at his clutch, but his hold was firm and protecting.

Jaryd had no choice but to throw her to the ground. She lay there seething at both Malik's killers and Jaryd's reluctance to let her fight as she so wished. Jaryd beckoned the nearest soldier over and removed his hand-scope from around his neck. With his sleeve, Jaryd gave the breastplate a brief polish and brought his scope in line with the soldier and the sacks that lay by the gate. The glass lenses of the scope concentrated and focussed the sun's streaming rays into a pencil-thin shaft of intense light, which hit and brilliantly illuminated a small spot on the side of one of the sacks.

Eva jumped up and held Jaryd's hands to further steady the scope and ensure the beam stayed on target. The sack smouldered and then burst into flame followed by the familiar sparks and red river of flame which engulfed the gate tracing out its matrix of metal. It was not long until the metal began to twist and crumble, and then finally break into falling pieces.

In Malik's absence, Jaryd raised his banner and waved a signal to Karel and Marcus, indicating that the gate's breach was imminent.

Karel moved directly to the wall and met Marcus's troops also traversing the perimeter to join Malik's men at the main gate, dodging and defending against the barrage of objects and arrows thrown and shot from above.

With the majority of Alvar's men still remaining defending the south wall and finding it difficult to negotiate the narrow ramparts to regroup nearer the gate, the rebellious army easily outnumbered the castle's defenders at the point of the breach and forced entry behind the outer walls.

The battle to enter the castle was won.

Alvar & Varga on the Offensive

"My lord." Alvar was observing with two of his generals and directing the battle from the high tower situated in the northeast corner of the castle walls. He had full view of the invading army as they broke through the first line of defence, but had not expected a direct assault on the heavy gate.

"What is it?" Alvar shouted.

"Word from the south is that the wooden tower is still moving to collide with the wall. There aren't many soldiers with it.

"And the main gate has been breached."

"You fool!" Alvar raised his baton and cracked it upon the messenger's head leaving a sharp cut. "I can see that. Take all men from the battlements and send them to protect the inner walls and repel these peasants."

"But that will leave the south unguarded against their wooden contraption," said the smaller of the two generals.

"That's just a decoy and probably always was," Alvar irritably replied, "and if you couldn't see that then you will be of more use on the front line. Go! Useless buffoon."

The humiliated general and the bruised messenger left the tower leaving Alvar with the remaining, slightly nervous general.

"And where are our mercenaries? We pay them enough. They should at least try to earn their money."

Alvar & Varga on the Offensive

"Perhaps they have decided it wiser to not take part in your fight. Maybe you should make a dignified exit too and retreat to battle another day."

Infuriated, Alvar again raised his broken baton but resisted. "Run away now you pathetic coward, before I throw you from the roof to die with your other useless soldiers."

The general, cowering with his forearm raised to defend his head, backed from the room, grateful to have not suffered a beating.

Alvar leaned forward to the tower's edge and peered down on his retreating army. "Absolutely useless."

In the courtyards and streets surrounding the inner walls, barricades had been erected to contain Marcus's advancing forces and prevent them from reaching Alvar's quarters.

The line of attackers stretched out over fifty men wide, with well-armed fighters at the front slicing and stabbing through Alvar's defensive lines. The attacking charge was fast and furious, and some of Alvar's men found themselves pushed through the surging assault and behind Marcus's frontmen. In this space, they could have the opportunity to attack the line's rear or flee through the gate. Regrettably, behind Marcus's front lines stood two or three more composed of farmers and workers wielding any implements they could carry. Mere farmers they may be, but their task was to pick out any stragglers, and this they accomplished with bludgeoning and hacking using clubs, scythes and wood-axes to great effect.

In less than an hour of close combat, Alvar's men were backed up tight to the inner wall, with only a single man deep keeping the invaders from crushing through and into the inner rooms. Dead from all sides lay scattered on the streets, but it was Alvar who had sustained the higher casualties.

Behind the lines, several older men and women from Marcus's force were tending and retrieving their wounded and carrying them to safety back through the main gate.

Both Jaryd and Eva were in the direct centre of the brawl. Both continued to wear their light armour, and Jaryd's recently donned spiked gauntlets were now covered with the dark blood of the enemy as he employed them to great effect pummelling into his opponents.

Jaryd's usual sword technique was to throw his sword at arm's length through the air in circular motions above his head, then lunge forward with devastating results on his target. The sword's razor-sharp orange-edged blade repeatedly cut deep on every strike, defeating his opponents regularly with a single blow, even through plate and mail.

With a short space between Eva and her fighting partner Jaryd, she was using two double-swords with competence and dexterity that would not usually be exhibited by even young men of her age. Her movement had a dance-like quality as her trim lithe figure would fouetté from one thrusting attack in front to another foe behind her. Using both swords and the hilts' dagger-length blades, her rapid twirling arm and body movements aided in mesmerizing her adversaries, leaving them disadvantaged for her final and fatal pounce.

Admittedly, Eva was fighting further from the doors that led to the inner castle chambers, and hence would have less experienced opponents to contend with. Nevertheless, she had sustained not a single cut. Jaryd, in contrast, was engaged directly in front of the main entrance to the castle buildings, and had suffered cuts to his forearm and cheek, blood running down his face and neck, dampening the collar of his tunic.

Alvar had repositioned himself within the halls and chambers of the inner sections of the castle. Although he could still directly observe the action close by the entrances, his messengers were providing the main detail about the battle's progress, and it wasn't good news.

His unused force's numbers still outweighed those of Marcus and he still had the upper hand as his waiting army was fresh and not battle-weary like the attackers. But he was not keen to test this premise. Alvar had another scheme that could not fail.

With the clamour of war surrounding him, it was proving challenging to request the attendance of his accomplice for his scheme to be realised. Precautions for his own safety, as he'd taken before, could not be prepared in these circumstances, but, since his own soul was already taken, there was little else he could lose. Varga's presence was called for.

Varga's form materialised immediately in front of Alvar taking him slightly by surprise. He had taken the appearance of a handsome army commander in full uniform, chest strewn with medals, a peaked hat, and a silver sword by his side. He had still not perfected the appearance of a human mouth, but his moustache covered, to some extent, his bared teeth. Varga could feel the death in the air and his skin tingled with excitement. The expression on his face was total rapture. Not only had he got Alvar in his grip and under control, but he could feast on the fresh souls of the dead to his heart's content.

"Looks like you need some help."

"Well, that was our agreement. Your assistance until my throne is secured." Alvar sounded a little desperate.

"And what would you like me to do? I can't just make them disappear you know."

"I hope you can offer something in return for my own soul which you didn't mind taking. Pull the souls from Jaryd, or Marcus, or all of them one by one." Alvar was certainly looking anxious.

"So many souls in healthy living bodies. Together with the requirement for close proximity to the intended target, that is a combination I deem to be too dangerous and will steer well clear of. But…"

"But what? You owe me." Desperate, anxious, and now impatient.

Varga looked out over the balcony. "There are many dead in the streets, dead from both sides of your war. Recently dead, with souls easily reachable."

His human face portrayed the concentration that was needed, and his outstretched arms and fingertips directed his thoughts and commandments. He was retrieving furious souls from withering into the dust and depositing them into the strewn bodies on the ground. Bodies that had recently lost their own souls, but may be able to live again with a little encouragement from Varga.

On the streets of battle, a sprawling dead soldier twitched. His fingers clinched the dry dirt on the ground and his eyelids snapped open revealing the whiteness of the rolled orbs. The man rose up, blood from his wounds still oozing and his broken leg remaining pointing in the wrong direction. The body could still function, but the mind was long gone and incapable of serious conscious thought. However, the remnants of a confused soul whose last objective was to fight and kill now reoccupied an animated body. Sword in hand the corpse-soldier faced the nearest living person and stumbled forward, swaying with each step, to fight once more.

Jaryd had made swift progress through the defence force and he, with the majority of his nearby allies, had reached the inner wall and main entrance. With the satisfying knowledge that Alvar's first line of defence had been eliminated, he was shocked and turned by a petrified cry from his rear. The panicked shouts were from several yards towards the outer wall, where the rear line of attack and the farmhands were standing.

He concentrated his stare through the ranks of men to determine the cause of the unrest.

"Eva, what do you see?" She lay one blade on her shoulder and held the other across her chest, retaining a defensive stance.

"It's more of Alvar's fighters. Can they have sprung from the ground or dropped in from above?" She looked hard to see any signs of once-buried trapdoors, or walkways above their heads, but none were present.

"Stay here!" Knowing that Eva had no intention of letting Jaryd venture towards these men alone, he made sure he was well in front of her giving as much protection as he could.

He pushed through his companions at arms who seemed only too willing to let him get closer. Then stopped and gaped at the sight of one of these new fighters. The combatant had his back facing Jaryd, and then a comrade's sword was thrust between his shoulder blades, deep into his back. The body turned wrenching the blade free and faced Jaryd directly. The man had a cold pale greying face which did not give the impression that he had received a serious injury. Another stab was made at this person's chest, again appearing to cause it no trouble. This was a walking dead.

Jaryd cast his eyes around and saw many other animated corpses tottering in to fight. Each being attacked by Marcus's men, and each not responding with any interest to the bodily injuries being inflicted.

The attacking force stepped back from these creatures, and then the fight started once more. With roles reversed, Marcus's men were now being pushed back. The renewed combat was intense and furious, but this new force held the upper hand. At that pace of attack, Marcus's army was going to be in serious trouble.

Jaryd relaxed his sword and stared into the dark eyes of an approaching soldier. Putting aside the information from his main senses, he peered into the man's soul using all the control he could muster. This body was finished just minutes before, but now it was reoccupied with another's soul, and this soul was determined to perform its previous duties.

Jaryd could see the soul and the desire it had to fight or go in peace. But the latter option was not being afforded it. This was some dirty sorcery being executed, and Jaryd felt sorrow and pity for the wayward souls.

He brought his senses back to the fore and felt a tear roll down his face. With a heavy heart and sadness flooding his mind, he raised his sword once more and then plunged it into his enemy. The man fell limp once more, sliding from Jaryd's blade. A shimmer of light remained fleetingly in the man's stead, the image of his soul, then evaporated to be finally at rest.

"These men are plagued with entrapped souls. Freedom from incarceration is by means of the orange metal, copper. Copper will repel the soul." Jaryd shouted to those close by. He lifted his sword and the copper-edged weapon glinted in the sunlight.

"We need to retreat. We are outnumbered by these unnatural beings."

Marcus took Jaryd's advice and signalled an orderly retreat to the outer walls. The order circulated to his men, and they cautiously retreated through the automatons, fending off their attacks. The assaults were relentless but slow and without a great deal of strength.

Alvar, with his deathly companion Varga, was observing Marcus's army being pushed back from his castle grounds. He snorted in amusement as he could see that this pathetic force was not a match for his skilled tactical play. And when he recognised some of the dead fighters as being from Marcus's own soldiers, he released a loud cackle of delight.

"Go on, go home, and take your dead, what's left of them, with you," Alvar shouted in the direction of the retreating forces.

"And remember that your strength pales into insignificance compared to my own powers," he taunted.

Marcus's men had withdrawn to just within the outer walls, but were not pursued further. An invisible barrier seemed to exist that brought Alvar's unnatural fighters to a halt. What remained of his living forces had dissipated during the recent fighting, not willing to partake or be the target of this fearless foe.

"Why are they stopping? Make them fight, rid my lands of these betrayers," Alvar commanded.

"Ah, my dear friend," Varga began, "everything has its limits, and my control, that's *my* control, does not extend to infinity. Perhaps you would like to join and lead your new army in the attack against Marcus. I must say, it would not be my favourite place to be."

Alvar, although not wholly satisfied with this outcome, was more or less content with the situation.

The attacking forces had been pushed back to the main gate and outer wall. All that remained was to direct his internal troops to depart by the south exits and rendezvous at the north gate to crush Marcus and his army between his own forces and the dead inside. A foolproof scheme, and victory would be his.

Jaryd ran to where Marcus was deliberating with his leaders. "This is not the work of Alvar alone. He has not the skill or powers to perform this hideous trick."

"Then who is assisting him? Does his wife have the necessary gifts?" Marcus asked.

"No! This is not the doing of a human. It can only be the product of the Lord of the dead, Varga." Jaryd began to explain. "The souls of the recently deceased are under the control of Varga, and have been re-entered into the soldiers you have just fought."

"That is disgusting. Have they no morality, Alvar or Varga?" Eva said as her face frowned in repulsion, "And how can these bodies still fight?"

"There is still some motive force available in even a dead body when it is controlled by another. Varga can control the physical form too when his obedient spirits have forced their way into the body. He can pump the heart and thus provide some limited energy.

"As for their morality, it would indeed seem that they do not possess such a quality.

"But there is a method to remove these entrapped souls and let them continue their own journeys, copper. When you need to confine a soul, place it in a copper-ringed flask. When it needs to be dispelled, put them into contact with copper." Jaryd's remarks made little sense to those around him. Only Jaryd's sword was tinged with this metal as ornate decoration. Was he to combat and restore this unnatural occurrence all by himself?

"Marcus, get your blacksmith to fire up his crucible. Melt down any copper pots you have, food bowls, cooking pots, everything." Jaryd's orders began to make sense. "We don't need to make new weapons, just a shallow coating produced by a swift immersion of your swords into the molten metal."

"We're grateful for your help. I just pray it'll work. Alvar has to be defeated."

"Varga too," added Jaryd.

Jaryd finds the King's Soul

"Jaryd, you're hurt." Eva winced as she looked at the gash on his face, and instinctively brought her fingertips up to his cheek and touched the cut.

He too reacted without thought and placed his hand on top of hers, pressing both flat onto his cheek.

There they remained for a few brief seconds then Jaryd lowered his touch down the back of her hand to her wrist and gently released her palm from his face. Their hands lowered and Eva's fingers slipped through Jaryd's slightly open hand.

He could see the concern in her eyes and calmingly said, "Don't worry. It's stopped bleeding. If that's all we end up with before our work is done, we'll be most thankful."

Tiana was at Marcus's side as he organised the blacksmith and his task of coating his force's weapons, when Jaryd and Eva walked up.

"Alvar is in collaboration with Varga, and he doesn't lend his hand for no reward," Jaryd remarked.

"When we were close to the inner wall, through all of the sadness and desperate cries from the ill-fated souls, I could feel the presence of Varga and the joy within him. That proves my theory of his assistance.

"What I could not detect, however, was the joy within Alvar's soul. Indeed, I had no sense of his soul at all."

Marcus listened intently and began to understand

what Jaryd was about to say.

"I believe the only reason," Jaryd continued, but sounding a little uncertain, "is that Alvar has had his soul taken, perhaps forcibly. Perhaps he is under the control of Varga. Whatever the exact circumstances, Alvar's soul is the key to the conclusion of our fight."

Eva knew what was coming next. "I have to find his soul. We have to find his soul." Jaryd looked directly at her knowing that what was about to happen would be the toughest test of her life.

"And do you know where it can be found?" Marcus asked. "Will he have it with him?"

"No, no. I don't believe so. He'll have it secured in his lair."

"And his lair, where is that?" Tiana added.

"In death."

"You're going into his realm to find the King's soul! How will you recognise it?" Marcus sounded worried for his friend.

"I don't think I can. There'll be thousands of indistinguishable essences all clamouring for their resting places. And what better place to hide something."

"You're not going! It'll take an eternity. You'll be lost."

"Thank you Eva, but I'm not going alone," he paused. "We have to talk." Jaryd's expression was the most serious she'd ever seen.

The couple found a quiet place within the surrounding trees and away from the commotion by the

Jaryd finds the King's Soul

blacksmith's fires. Marcus had sent Tiana and a small squad of men with them for protection, but they were stationed out of earshot.

"I had no idea how I was ever going to tell you this. Maybe I would never have told you, but now there is no escape," Jaryd started.

"You are the daughter of two most experienced and respected sorcerers and friends. King Godwyn and," he hesitated. Was it really necessary to tell her the whole truth? He continued, "Annea, she was your mother. I'm so sorry."

Eva knew she'd heard correctly, but could it be true? So many thoughts and memories were flooding Eva's mind. She remembered so much, so quickly. Times with Annea, her mother. Memories of the King, the King and Annea, were too much to understand.

She wanted to run. Just run away to be safe from this confusing situation. Hide and cry. But to her own amazement, she did not. She stood motionless still looking at Jaryd, waiting for him to say it'll be alright. Simply wanting him to take all the turmoil away, simply wanting him to put everything back to normal. But in the same way a child cannot have their favourite broken toy repaired by words, she knew this was part of her life that would need to be resolved, in time, by herself alone.

Jaryd stepped closer, not knowing whether to embrace her and comfort her. He wanted to. He wanted to so much, but not now.

"Your locket." Jaryd pointed to the chain around her neck. "I think it will open now."

Eva looked down and pulled the locket from within her tunic, placing the silver disc in her hand. She stared at it, at the pentagonal royal design, and realised she was crying both tears of sadness and those of the deepest joy. With her head still bowed, tears rolled down her nose and dripped onto the locket's face. There was a small click, and from the side of the ornament, a round button appeared.

She wiped her tears from her face with her fingers, and pressed the button releasing the locket's covers and slowly opened it. Inside were two paintings. On the left-hand side, a picture of Annea, Godwyn and a small baby cradled between them in her arms. On the right, a softly smiling portrait of her mother.

She stared at both pictures, touching them with her fingertips, wanting them to be real. Then closed it revealing the engraving *To my dear daughter* on the back. She understood it now, it had always been a gift for her.

Jaryd led the party deeper into the forest, Eva following behind with Tiana and her troops protecting the rear. The trees were forming dense walls around them and their canopies shielded them from the early evening daylight. The ground was covered with a variety of rotting leaves and pine needles, forming a soft carpet on which to quietly walk. There were no sounds of battle here, only the distant birdsong high above gave them any comfort.

"Is this not far enough?" Tiana called to Jaryd. "We are far from reach of Alvar's forces."

"If I have tracked correctly, we'll be there very soon."

"Eva," Jaryd spoke quietly for none but her to hear, "you know why you're here with me?"

"Because you swore to my mother that you'd protect me." Eva was gaining confidence in referring to Annea as her mother, and in doing so, it gave her warmth in her heart.

"Well, that's partly true. I made a promise that I will do my utmost to keep, a promise to care for you. A promise that'll be a pleasure to fulfil."

"Looks like you're the one that needs looking after," she replied pointing to the cut on his face.

Eva's jest brought a smile and a laugh from Jaryd, and lightened the mood in this grave situation. Whether she thought it appropriate or not, Eva walked closer to Jaryd and took his hand in hers.

"It seems that you're stuck with me then."

Shafts of bright yellow light spilt through the branches and trunks ahead of them, bathing the group in the warm autumn sun. They were nearing a clearing in the trees and it was becoming eerily quiet, no birdsong, not even the sound of the breeze rustling in the leaves. It was a deathly hush.

The party shortly stepped into full light and into a circular clearing populated by several man-high monoliths arranged regularly around what looked as if it had once been an altar at the centre. The earth here was dark, damp and bare. The stones bore dark stains which were a testament to the sinister performances carried out in this place.

"Is it, safe here?" Tiana questioned Jaryd's choice of location.

"You are too young to remember first-hand, and it's unlikely that the stories of events carried out here would be passed down. This place is being forgotten, and rightly so."

Tiana accompanied Eva walking around the central stone, running their hands over the cold surface and imagining what took place here many, many years earlier.

"Are you going to explain more?" She pushed for some further information.

"As I say, this place is being forgotten, and I do not believe there is any need for additional detail. Many men, women and children visited this place, and did not leave. If I say that the path into death is well-trodden here, I think you'll understand.

"Due to this location's history, the barrier between this world and that of the dead is fragile, unused now, but it will be our entry point."

"Our entry point," Eva repeated in her head. She didn't need to ask what "our" meant. She unbuckled her belts and removed her swords handing them to Tiana. "Shall we go?" Her words were shaky and full of emotion.

Jaryd removed his sword and cloak and laid them on the stone altar. He then took a small bag from around his neck, opened it and set out the contents on the ground.

"This will speed our departure." Jaryd bent down and opened two small bottles letting the coloured smoke infuse the air and surround the travellers.

He stood opposite Eva and offered both his hands to her which she readily took. They were warm but her palms were sweaty in expectation. The smoke was curling around their faces. Eva had her mouth tightly closed and was breathing shallow breaths.

"You must breathe deeply, it is not an unpleasant odour. Open your mouth and fill your lungs. Discard your chains of common sense and offer me your heart, your mind, and your soul."

Eva took in one long breath pushing her chest out and raising her shoulders, held it for a moment, and then exhaled slowly letting her body relax.

"That's it, keep going," Jaryd urged.

She took in another breath. Her senses swam and her head fell back with her eyes closed. She straightened up and the next exhalation was slow, steady and gentle, and then she settled into a more relaxed rhythm.

After a few more breaths she could feel life leaving her legs. The muscles in her calves tensed, and then the sensation rose up to her thighs, groin and into her chest.

Eva could not see nor hear Jaryd in front of her, but still had the remaining sense of touch in her hands, and could feel his warm palms against her own which were growing colder as her life-force ran from her body through her fingertips and into her travelling companion.

As the last drops of her essence departed her human form, all of her bodily senses ceased to exist. She felt absolute contentment and was totally at ease with all she had recently learnt and suffered. Eva felt no sorrow for not knowing Annea as her mother, or that Godwyn was her father. She was totally at peace.

Jaryd was regrettably all too familiar with the sensation of leaving life on the journey into death, but had to travel fast as Eva's soul was only loosely held in his possession once again.

The journey was short, as predicted by Jaryd. He correctly assumed that the barrier between the two worlds would be thin at this point, and soon the pair of souls were in death.

Maintaining complete control and possession of a soul in life, other than your own, required a mastery of this art. To be in charge of your own soul in death was difficult and fraught with dangers. Attempting to carry another for any length of time was utterly impossible for a person with an existent human form in life, as a soul connected by a thread to a living body acts like a magnet to the inhabitants of that world.

Jaryd's translation into this place was complete, and then he spilt his delicate load from his mind into another separate human-like form, but retained a tenuous connection through their connected hands for guidance and protection.

"Are you ok?" Eva could not see his lips or mouth moving, but instead, his words simply formed inside her mind.

He could see that she was obviously frightened by the experience as she had not yet attempted to probe any further than Jaryd with her mind.

"Don't be alarmed by your surroundings and those

Jaryd finds the King's Soul

that dwell within them. I'll not let anything harm you. And please do not let go of my arm." His instruction and reassurance worked, and after a brief pause, Eva opened her eyes and mind to this new environment.

To her, this place appeared dark and chilling. She could witness the travelling souls, but could not feel their sorrow as Jaryd could. Distressed, the arm-to-arm bond between the adventurers weakened as she started to lose concentration.

"Eva! Look at me," Jaryd said. "Concentrate and hold me tight. In the event that we may become separated, make your way as best you can to this point." He pointed at a star-bright orange glow which appeared to be emanating from a silver shaft protruding from the ground. Jaryd did not need to leave a marker as he had always needed to do in the past. For here, the strength of his sword's coating was sufficient to pierce into their new world, acting like a beacon to life.

Eva looked at the sword's light and then back to Jaryd. The bond tightened, and where their arms met, a blue light shone gently. Jaryd had never seen this before, then again, he'd never taken another's soul here as a travelling companion. The light looked cool but felt warm, and seemed to bond them tightly. He could not explain it.

"I know where Varga's lair is, but when we reach that place, I am not going to be able to locate Alvar's soul. That, my dear, is your task." With the dangers of their current predicament, Jaryd could only think about why he had used such a stupid expression. "My dear" would be a term used for his old grandmother, not for a young woman who was inappropriately occupying more and more of his thoughts.

He wanted to break the bond to keep some privacy of his thoughts, but he did not get the sense that Eva wanted to reciprocate. Perhaps these notions had not been conveyed, or perhaps they had been accepted.

He snapped his mind back to the task at hand, and pulled Eva along with him against the flow of souls by their feet.

"Shouldn't we be following these spirits to Varga's lair? Isn't that where they finally go to rest?"

"Normally, yes. But these poor creatures are being recalled as we saw earlier. They are actually travelling from his lair. It'll be harder going, but at least they will act as a compass to where his home is."

"Can they hurt us? Can we hurt them?"

"Yes. Unlikely, but yes. They are currently being set on a different task and should ignore our presence. Just try and move smoothly and slowly. Their essence can be torn, and we should respect all of them and try to do no harm."

It was indeed slow progress through the strong tide of spirits surging past their feet and back into life. Eva and Jaryd shuffled cautiously on their journey and only accidentally split one soul. It wasn't a major tear, and the injured soul quickly repaired itself as it squirmed around their legs, letting out a small squeal as it did so.

"Do you feel anything within these souls?" Jaryd asked.

"I feel a sort of confusion, I think. I'm not sure if it's my own state of mind that I'm feeling, or that I'm really sensing the suffering of these souls."

"And are you confused here?"

"I guess not. I mean, I don't understand it all, but that's probably a lack of experience."

"So you're teaching yourself. You now know that you can 'feel' the souls. Feel them in your mind. Practise, and try and feel deeper into each soul's state."

Jaryd looked about and then placed his foot gently, but firmly, onto the tail of a meandering essence.

"Look at this one. Tell me, what can you feel?"

Eva stared down past their joined arms and under his foot. The essence of this one was struggling with little effort and simply managing to wrap around his ankle forming a shape like a doughnut.

"I have a sense of tiredness, resentment too. I think resentment is quite an abundant sensation down here."

"That's undeniable. All of the souls flowing in the wrong direction feel that they should be left in peace. Even those of our enemy who had been slain in battle, they all need to rest."

"And the tiredness?" Eva was inquisitive about learning more about this talent.

"The one here, around my foot, is of an old man who wishes to be at rest. He has been here too long to delve any deeper into his previous life, and will not make a good occupant of Alvar's living dead."

Soul Thieves

Jaryd continued to test Eva's emerging ability, asking questions about the lessening number of passing souls. She had really gained a good understanding of the basic moods that could be perceived, but the number of passing souls became fewer as Varga's lair got closer.

"I'm not going to be able to help you with the next part of this venture. As the only known living blood relative, and with the unfortunate closeness you have to him, think deeply about your uncle. What was he like? What emotions would he be feeling? Choose an emotion that may feel out of place here. That will make him easier to locate."

Eva thought of all the negative points of Alvar, maliciousness, thoughtlessness, and selfishness. There were just too many, but these were all, what Jaryd had called, 'dark emotions'. She had to find something that would be out of place here. Something that she could tune into amongst the other trapped beings.

"Happiness!" Eva shouted aloud. "Surrounded by all of this death, Alvar's soul would be the one that would feel the most pleasure."

Jaryd was impressed. He had been laboriously searching the neighbouring souls, one by one, and had not once felt any happiness. Of course, he had felt their contentment on previous visits, but never any signs of joy. That was such an out-of-place emotion in this land that it just had to be the correct aim.

Eva too was pleased, and grinned widely.

"Don't cloud your feelings with that of your own," Jaryd said.

Jaryd finds the King's Soul

Her grin faded and she realised Jaryd had pulled her to a halt. In front, and around them, was a raised area of ground. No souls were here, but the ground still moved inexplicably. On this mound were chests. Not solid structures that she was used to, but thick dark clouds that had neither walls nor lids. But they were still without doubt containers.

"Jaryd, there are hundreds of boxes, do I have to open them all?"

"Actually, no. That would not be a good idea. Whilst Varga would not have booby-trapped these, it is most likely that some of the contents would not be best pleased with seeing us, or anyone else for that matter."

They crept amongst the many chests, trying to determine the contents by willpower alone.

"I don't want to put you under too much stress, but we might only have one chance." This was a severely dangerous situation, and Jaryd was attempting to lessen the seriousness with typical Jaryd humour. "Have a look around."

It was a daunting task for Eva. She'd only just started on the road to becoming a seer like Jaryd, and now she had to do something that he couldn't. She stopped in her slow search and craned her neck forward, squinting with both eyes. "It's there, I'm sure it is. The red box."

Jaryd moved to where she was standing looking in the direction that Eva's free hand was pointing. He couldn't see it so moved closer to her face to see exactly what she saw. It was still not visible to him.

She pulled Jaryd from where he stood and they

dashed to the box she had chosen. "This one."

She knelt by her box. To Jaryd, it looked just like all of the others, dull, cloudy and black.

"How do you open it?" Eva sounded so confident it would not be possible to tell that she was only a beginner.

"You lift one end and I'll lift the other. But be careful. If it's a powerful enraged and hungry spirit, then, well, run!"

He looked at her. Apart from the glowing bonded arms hanging between them as they crouched by the box, Jaryd felt an unusual attachment to her.

"Eva, I…"

She turned to him and raised her eyebrows questioningly.

"I… I'll count to three. One, two."

On the count of three, they raised the box's lid and fell backwards, putting out their hands behind to prevent them from falling flat on the ground.

They sat there and stared, nothing happened.

Their eyes were level with the opening to the box so they could not see into it without sitting up and moving closer.

Peering over the edge, Jaryd was still unable to discern this spirit from any others that he had previously encountered. But, submitting to Eva's continued words of excited confirmation, he put his hand in and extracted the flimsy essence, entrapping it as he had done with Eva's only a week earlier.

"How does it feel?" Eva asked.

"It's cold. This spirit has no desires except for revenge

Jaryd finds the King's Soul

against his brother and his supporters." He hoped his reference to Eva's father would not distract her from their journey back to life.

Eva too could feel the presence of Alvar's soul within their two bodies. For her, it was uncomfortable and nauseating. She wanted the occupation to end immediately.

Jaryd stood tall and looked in the direction of their entry into this world and located a strangely distant orange glow illuminating their exit. But, between where he stood and the edge of the raised mound, another smaller chest drew his attention. This chest was hiding in the shadow of many larger adjacent ones, and it only stood out in Jaryd's mind by its sheer diminutive size. It was actually unbelievably darker than the surrounding chests.

They approached it and uncharacteristically Jaryd was uncontrollably overcome with the need to open the box. He knelt and opened it without considering the consequences, or trying to see the contents. Eva too had no time to prevent him.

At the bottom of the small box was an even smaller spirit or fragment. Jaryd regained some restraint and prodded it, feeling and seeing it through his fingers. If that soul which he had just extracted and carried within him was cold, this one was the lord of all pitiless, cold-hearted creatures.

It was part of Varga himself.

Alvar is Defeated

Small skirmishes continued around the main gate of Alvar's castle as a few of his brave soldiers fought through the animated dead fighters under Varga's control. Varga's army was confined to within the walls where they were in sight of, and within range of Varga's power. With a little more determination and bravery on his part, he could advance his forces still further.

From out of the south gates Alvar commanded the majority of his unused fighters to attack directly into Marcus's forces.

Marcus's own men were much lower in number, and taking into account that Tiana was not present and had taken some experienced men with her, the allied forces were heavily outnumbered.

The blacksmith's crucible was glowing bright orange under the intense heat forced into it by teams of bellows operators straining to pump air into the fire. Within this, a crust-covered molten mass of metal was waiting.

The smithy swept over the surface and removed the slag revealing the bright liquid copper and then signalled to Marcus that it was ready.

An organised line of men formed with swords ready. As each walked past the smithy's fire, they briefly submerged the tips of their weapons into the liquid, withdrawing them with a bright copper coating which would hopefully overcome the un-dead of Varga.

After just a few minutes, Marcus had assembled a

couple of dozen men prepared to advance back through the gates and engage Varga's fighters.

Karel rode over to Marcus. "There's an army approaching from the south wall. It'll be here in just a few minutes." Karel was in his element now, a professional fighter.

"We don't have the capacity to fight with you," he continued, "but we'll stand in their way and give you as much time as we can. You have to go through the gate now."

They clapped each other on the shoulder with a recognition that neither might survive this final assault.

"To the gate!" Marcus cried.

Karel despatched a dozen men to run in front of Marcus's troops, and the remainder formed a three-rank deep line of armour that steadily marched towards Alvar's attacking force.

As both Marcus's and Karel's groups neared the walls they engaged the opposition, rendering Alvar's archers on the parapets useless, lest they fire upon their own kind.

Alvar had always intended to use his archers, whether they hit the opposition or not, but Varga held him back. "It doesn't worry me, but you do have to live with these people after the war is won. And it would be better to have them as loyal as you can hope for."

Alvar shrugged his shoulder but abided by Varga's advice, the archers were stood down.

They had not moved from the balcony from where they had overlooked Varga's resurrected men thwart

Marcus's initial attack on his inner walls. They could see that Marcus had now fought his way back through the gate, through Alvar's men that had pursued him earlier, and were again fighting Varga's army. Alvar's men still refused to follow the small group of attackers.

Alvar's grin was slowly removed as he observed the progress Marcus was making through the supposedly unstoppable creatures.

"Varga, your army is being hacked down. How can this be?"

Resuming his attack in the inner courtyard, Marcus and his small group of men were using their newly coated swords with devastating effect. Every thrust into the torso of an opponent would create an ear-splitting screech and a wisp of smoke from the wound. The re-embodied spirits were forced to depart by the copper metal repelling the inhuman occupiers, and the corpses fell back to the ground.

Progress against Varga's men was swift. Marcus and his human attackers were less numerous than their opponents, but had an agility that easily surpassed that of the lumbering controlled monsters.

The inner wall was soon reached, but with the demise of Varga's force, Alvar's small army battling a short distance from the gate entered to fight at Marcus's rear.

Karel had manoeuvred his followers between the assaulting force from the south exits, and those at the main gate, now forming a complex sandwich comprising Marcus at the inner wall, then Alvar's small force, followed by Karel and then the far larger opposing force

Alvar is Defeated

still arriving from the south.

All of Karel's might was targeted at securing a safe passage from the woods and to the gate. This path would be where Jaryd would need to travel and combat Alvar, but the path was being narrowed, restricted by the surge of Alvar's forces, sealing off the entrance and exit to the castle.

The push from both sides continued as Karel lost even more ground. From his mounted position he glanced back to the woods. A hurried movement caught his attention. Quickly into view charged half a dozen mounted soldiers bearing the insignia of Marcus's guard. Leading the group was Tiana, but Jaryd nor Eva were following. What was giving chase was a detail of Alvar's soldiers and scouts, hotly pursuing their quarry.

Karel's heart sank to a depth of complete defeat. Tiana's position in the deep woods must've been uncovered, and Jaryd had been left behind, Tiana only just escaping defeat herself.

Tiana rode up the short path to the gate and was not going to halt when she reached Karel. Aloft in the air, she brandished a long sword as if making a last-ditch attack.

The sword shone, not a gleaming silver, but a yellow-brown tinged glow emanating from the point. This was Jaryd's sword.

"Make way, make way," Karel shouted, and he forged a path for Tiana to travel.

Her group thundered past the foot soldiers from both sides and entered the castle grounds. Behind them,

Karel's ranks closed in preventing the pursuers from following.

As Tiana reached the inner wall doors, parting Marcus's soldiers as she rode, her horse came to a sliding halt and reared up onto its hind legs. Pawing its hooves in the air, they came crashing down upon the wooden door splintering it from its hinges and letting it fall to the marble floor with a crash.

Alvar looked on as the feeble girl broke into his castle, Varga at his side.

"Don't be afraid my friend," Varga said. "I can feel the weakness of her soul, she is alone, brave but weak. She won't cause you any problem."

Tiana rode on, her billowing cloak covering her horse's rear quarters. She entered into the castle rooms which were strangely deserted, then made her way past the staircase that lead to the balcony and Alvar, and onto wooden floors in a much older part of the castle.

She had a destination firmly fixed in her mind and raced through narrowing corridors towards the old prayer hall. This was a very much unused part of the building and the boards creaked and flexed under the hooves of her horse.

She trotted carefully over the dusty floor, ducking down to avoid cobwebs hanging between rafters illuminated by shafts of light cutting through high narrow windows.

At the end of this passage, a small door opened easily leading to an ornate prayer hall. Rows of benches were laid out facing an elaborate stained glass window

Alvar is Defeated

decorated with doves flying above deep green grass. Unlit torches were positioned between the windows on one side, and the other displayed tapestries and paintings of previous kings.

Alvar had no use of this place and it was left to ruin, but beneath the floor lay the crypt, and a direct path out of this world.

Tiana, still mounted, released her cloak for it to remain draped on her horse, gained full movement of her arms and body, and raised Jaryd's sword in her outstretched arm high above her head. With a single swift movement, she spun the sword in her palm to point to the floor and thrust the blade down splintering through the stiff wooden boards and embedding the orange tip below the floor.

Two pairs of arms and leather-gloved hands seem to have appeared from nowhere on either side of Tiana. Alvar's guards struggled for a moment but quickly manhandled her from her seat and forced her to the floor. With her own sword tucked into her horse's saddle and now concealed by her cloak, she was left unarmed facing, not just the guards, but the King who steadily walked into the room followed by his cohort Varga.

"Well, well. This is indeed a peculiar way to attempt to assassinate your King." Alvar could taste victory now. Not only were the attackers outnumbered, he now had the queen-in-waiting as hostage.

He walked towards Jaryd's sword which was gently swaying erect from the floor. "You seem to have dropped your weapon. Very careless." He had not seen

Tiana deliberately place the sword and did not see her other in her saddle.

"This is a strange place to search for me. Did you expect that I'd be praying in the heat of the battle?" He ordered his guards to push her onto her knees. They held her arms straight out behind her and forced her shoulders forward, head bowed.

With a splintering screech, Alvar tugged and removed Jaryd's sword. He raised its tip in front of his face and considered it to be a heavy object for such a slight woman.

"Ingenious." He twirled the blade whilst looking at the copper point. "I do hope it's sharp. Any last requests?"

Tiana stared into Alvar's dark eyes but said nothing. She would not betray anyone, and was not afraid of this pitiful man.

"Let her go!"

"What?" Alvar spun round and lowered the sword. Jaryd stood amongst a couple of Hessian sacks and a discarded cloak where they had quietly descended from Tiana's horse. He stood several paces from Alvar with Eva close by, bowstring drawn and ready. She had an emotionless stare fixed upon the guards restraining Tiana. "How did you get here?"

"That's my sword. Please." He held out his hand for its return and took a step closer to Tiana as the guards strengthened their grip and pushed her back further down. Eva loosed an arrow that flew past Jaryd and directly into the helmet of the closest guard. His hands

Alvar is Defeated

tightened, blood started to flow between his eyes, then he released Tiana's arm and fell to one side dead. Eva's bow was already prepared for another shot before the remaining guard even had time to stand. He released Tiana instinctively to defend himself. As his right hand moved towards his sword Eva's arrow hit him in the throat, immobilising him instantly. He fell to his knees clutching the arrow's shaft and gurgled before toppling forward.

"Very impressive girl. But your little arrows won't hurt me."

Tiana lay curled up on the floor. She was in shock but otherwise unharmed. In the instant Eva glanced down at her friend, relaxing her concentration from the task in hand, Varga stepped forward and pulled at her soul with his outstretched fingers.

The whiteness of Eva's skin began to darken and turn a light grey as wisps of her soul started to depart her body. She staggered and her bow fell to the ground. Jaryd grabbed her hand and their souls instantly bonded once more. His strength and familiarity with her spirit effortlessly allowed him to counter Varga's attempt.

Jaryd caught Eva's unconscious body as Varga relinquished his attack, and laid it gently on the floor.

Varga steadied himself after his failed attempt to take Eva's life once and for all. He stood, visibly annoyed at Jaryd's interference, contemplating his next move. Jaryd's soul was complete and was almost certainly strong-willed. Strong enough to repel a direct attack.

Jaryd too stood facing his opponents, prepared to

defend himself, but he considered that he had the upper hand, and withdrew a small bottle from his pocket.

"Isn't this a strange situation? Here we have the lord of souls who had promised to look after little Alvar's prize possession." Whether he would be victorious or not, Jaryd decided to ridicule the pair as much as he could, and possibly throw them off balance. "And what do you think I have here?"

Alvar looked at the bottle in Jaryd's hand, then at Varga's face for confirmation that it was not what he thought it was. He could not feel its contents, but Varga could.

"Thief! That's not yours to take." Varga's exclamation was the confirmation that Alvar did not want to hear. "The realm of death is mine to control, and you have trespassed like so many others."

"You are mistaken and misguided. Your rite to command all souls is not a valid claim. No one being holds that position, least of all you. You have misdirected too many spirits beyond even your reach, so I claim this," Jaryd held out the bottle, "in recompense."

Alvar turned in desperation to Varga, but Varga was unsure where this was leading. He really could have more to lose than Alvar. Alvar was essentially lost already, and Jaryd was not just an apprentice like Eva.

Sweat was forming on Alvar's brow, and his lips trembled. "We, we could rule together. Unstoppable. You'd have everything you desire."

Jaryd ignored his mad suggestions. "I have felt and heard the screams from within these walls too many times. For them, for Annea, for the countless others you have tortured, you cannot continue."

Without a hint of remorse for his intended action, Jaryd pulled the stopper from the bottle and turned it over. Alvar's thin liquid-like spirit flowed quickly to the ground only too eager to go to rest.

"Trap it, stop it you fool," Alvar shouted at Varga as he rushed to Jaryd's feet and scraped his fingers at the cracks in the floor. With Varga in life, Alvar's soul would travel to the far end of death, and his body would drop.

"You son of a..." Alvar stood and drew a dagger from his side and lunged towards Jaryd. "You can join me."

Jaryd sidestepped the attack, but Alvar quickly turned and stabbed at his back. He abruptly stopped short and the dagger fell from his open hand to the floor. Alvar looked down at his chest. Eva was standing close behind him holding Jaryd's sword, the sharp point protruding blood-stained through Alvar's ribs. She reached her free hand towards Alvar's head and pulled his hair back, sliding his body towards hers, to the sword's hilt, and whispered through gritted teeth, "No body, no soul. Rot in hell!"

Alvar's body slid from the sword, and Jaryd looked towards Eva. She had a look of satisfied revenge upon her face, and tears of relief in her eyes.

"Your lair holds secrets that you supposed could not be uncovered."

Varga did not reply, but stood motionless.

"I have tasted your soul. I can feel your presence in

this world like a nauseating pain in my stomach. What do you consider to be your most prized possession?"

Jaryd quickly calculated that the part-soul that he retrieved from Varga's lair was the mechanism by which Varga could easily navigate death. A marker and beacon for the return to his lair.

"I have not decided your fate. I wonder if you could find what I carry if it were to be released free into your world, and went the same way as that poor soul." Jaryd pointed at the body of the late King.

"You are becoming a trifle tiresome, and your proposed action would only be a minor hindrance. I will retrieve my full soul, then we'll see who has the last laugh."

"Then I suggest you go back home and wait for your soul to come floating by." Jaryd had no intention of disposing of his stolen prize yet. Varga would simply depart, recover what had been stolen, and then return moments later, fully restored and ready to duel.

"There is now room in the soul canister for another occupant." Jaryd held out the empty bottle that had contained Alvar's essence as a threat to Varga. The bottle remained primed and ready to perform again.

"I can wait," Varga said.

"You don't have any other choice."

Varga's form simply vanished leaving Jaryd, Eva and Tiana alone, but in victory.

Jaryd turned to face the two women. Tiana was standing unhurt. "We were ambushed, in the clearing. I

Alvar is Defeated

didn't know what to do."

"You made a wise decision, and a brave move to come here. This crypt is very close to the dead."

Still trembling after despatching Alvar, with his blood covering her hands, Eva ran unsteadily to Jaryd and crashed into his body, burying her face in his chest. Her hands clenched tight upon his lapels. She did not want to let go.

He moved his hands from waist level, without touching her, and gently but firmly squeezed her upper arms, holding her without any concern for propriety, and kissed her hair.

Eva had stopped shaking and was savouring the moment of closeness as Tiana approached. She thought about releasing Eva's arms and taking her away from this place, to somewhere quiet, but stopped short of pulling her away. She smiled at Jaryd and left, picking up Alvar's sword symbolic of his defeat.

Ophilya, Nasty!

"Do you think it's wise Marcus?" Jaryd asked. "Ophilya is the deposed queen and we do not fully understand her motives and what her allegiances are."

Marcus had considered this question many times before inviting Ophilya to the castle at Abeline. She had disappeared before the battles and there was no solid news as to her whereabouts. From what Jaryd could glean from his brief time as her prisoner, she did have plans to return in the near future. This she had explicitly said and also hinted that it would be without Alvar too.

She did have a small group of followers and mercenaries of her own. That much was widely known. But now, she had no real power. No real chance of returning in any capacity as she once had. Well, time would tell.

Alvar's old meeting room was filled by Marcus, Jaryd and several of Marcus's closest allies and advisors. Eva sat at the opposite side of the room to Jaryd, a vacant seat positioned as their focus directly beside Marcus. Their talents for seeing into the soul would be useful here, and two seers were better than one.

The door opened and everyone stood. Ophilya entered determinedly into the chamber acknowledging the greetings of the others present. Marcus warmly welcomed her and directed her to the empty seat. Ophilya stopped and turned to the door.

Ophilya, Nasty!

"Please, may I introduce Haram?" The clerik stood, attired not in the traditional clerik's robes, but more stylishly even than Marcus.

Karel stood and offered his seat next to Ophilya's. Jaryd and Eva exchanged glances which Karel spotted. But it was too late. His seat was occupied. He had acted with impeccable manners but had seated Haram, an experienced seer, immediately beside Ophilya blocking direct sight from Jaryd. There was nothing that could be done now. Karel stood behind Marcus with an apologetic expression on his face. Seeing into Ophilya's mind would be far more testing now with only Eva in a direct line.

The gathering started to return to their seats amidst mild murmurs of perceptible disapproval. Karel sat behind Marcus on a chair provided by a standing waiter.

"Thank you for agreeing to this summit." Ophilya was first to speak, and as she did so the room quietened.

Marcus remained silent but nodded awkwardly. They were, until very recently, enemies. But he was curious as to what she had planned.

"Introductions over, now let's get straight to business and my proposals."

Marcus was visibly taken aback at Ophilya's opening sentence. The usual attention to the rules of diplomacy was absent. At least the exchange should be frank.

"Please continue," Marcus said, knowing that she had every intention of doing so without his consent.

"Abeline is my home, I know the people here, and Haram has been teaching for many years before that. We two should rule here. You have Wodel's interests still to manage."

"You have only been present here a few years. There are many others, even within this room, that have more regard for the nature of the people of Abeline." Marcus's reply indicated to Ophilya that negotiations would be tough and her suggestion would need to be fought out. "Why should we not choose Jaryd as ruler? He has respect, has lived here longer and…"

"But with all respect to your friend, he is from a despised clerik family. And there should be two on the throne, he has no queen." Eva fidgeted in her chair.

"And your partner is from a respected clerik upbringing?" Marcus countered.

"He has not hidden what he believes in." The heat in Ophilya's voice was growing, and the conversation was becoming bitter and personal. An acceptable solution was seemingly going to be hard to reach.

Out of sight of the two guests Jaryd signalled to Eva. The noise in the room was rising and arguments were breaking out. So much for the little diplomacy that had existed.

Eva closed her eyes and slipped into a deeply relaxed state. Jaryd's teachings of technique and purpose were learnt well. She quickly muted the background noise from her thoughts and released her mind to travel the room.

There were strong presences in the room. She felt Jaryd's which she easily recognised, and Marcus was visible too. There were two others, hardly separable, that tugged at her attention. These Eva assumed were those of Ophilya and Haram.

It was Haram's thoughts and feelings that were her target, but not directly. An attempt to examine his soul would unquestionably be detected. Instead, Eva concentrated her endeavours on Ophilya's mind and spirit. She would hopefully have the whole plan buried in her thoughts.

Visions were popping into her mind. Ophilya's contempt for her husband, the loss of his finger, and their wedding day. All entertaining information but none of it any use here. Their minds wandered, entwined until the shapes of a cloaked and hooded man materialised. It was Haram, and they were in discussion. Plans were being drawn, and inhuman creations were being discussed, but these were only outlines. Eva needed to delve deeper to extract the detail.

"No, you don't little girl."

The strong features of Haram's face were perfectly focused in Eva's mind. She stared into his eyes. It felt too real. She forced herself back to reality and the living world and unquiet in the room. Haram was staring at her, a slight smile rising on his mouth.

Eva tried to break their locked eyes but couldn't. Her breathing became forced and shallow, and she started to panic and sweat, glistening beads forming on her forehead. She was suffocating.

Jaryd saw the distress on Eva's face, but could not see Ophilya's or Haram's. He knew she was in danger.

As the debate raged without clear direction Jaryd stood. "Perhaps it's time for some private discussions."

He walked into the centre of the room and broke the connection between Eva and her attacker. Eva gasped a deep breath and began shallow panting trying to recover her composure.

"There is no need for privacy here. We've been completely open and honest," Ophilya declared.

Eva stood.

"No, you haven't been totally truthful," Eva spoke through a swirling mass of thoughts. She didn't know what else to say, and ran from the room dizzy with emotion.

Many others were now standing and Jaryd took the opportunity to follow Eva. She stood just outside the entrance leaning and holding onto a wooden post, gently sobbing. Jaryd approached and rested a hand on her shoulder.

She looked at Jaryd. She recalled her mother's advice about not becoming a sorcerer, getting married instead and having a family. That path would've been so much easier and safer.

"What happened?" Jaryd spoke softly.

"I saw a plan. A plan with inhuman creations. Then Haram was there, he tried to kill me." Eva was breathing steadily and calming down as Jaryd continued to hold her shoulder.

"You were brave and strong," Jaryd reassured her. "Were these creations the same as we fought outside the castle? Souls placed into the dead."

Ophilya, Nasty!

"No, this was different. Souls were part of the creation, but there were no bodies involved," Eva answered. "I got the feeling that Haram was not happy with the plan, but he seemed trapped by his desires."

"So Ophilya and Haram are not just partners in this crime, but lovers too?"

Eva nodded in agreement.

"We shall have to see how events transpire. I suspect we will know soon enough. Wait here and enter when you're ready." Jaryd walked away and entered the discussions once more.

Ophilya stood her ground and asked again, "Do you agree that Haram and myself should rule Abeline?"

"That just isn't appropriate for the people of this city. I'm sorry," Marcus concluded.

"You will be sorry. Haram, move!" Ophilya angrily shouted her instruction and stepped away from Marcus pushing Haram towards the door.

Marcus outstretched his arms in a pleading gesture but suddenly took a step back as Ophilya removed some objects from her gown and placed them on the floor.

The objects were round, about the size of an orange, and shone brightly in the window light. The upper half of the sphere was not solid metal, but glass domed and criss-crossed with copper strands. Jaryd looked at the globes laying motionless on the floor and saw through the glass to the contents inside.

He felt a presence. A small feeling of something inhuman. These were the creations Eva saw in her examination of Ophilya's mind. He recognised the contents. They were squirming essence, but not of men.

Half a dozen jointed protrusions erupted from the bottom half of the objects and extended several inches like spidery legs, clicking upon the stone floor as they felt their new surroundings, and lifting their bodies clear of the ground.

"Haram, now!" Ophilya commanded.

Haram raised his hands, and with a swift sweeping motion, the spheres moved into action. Four small mechanical creatures probed the floor, turning trying to identify their prey, and centred on Marcus backing towards the wall.

A guard jumped forward blocking the machine's advance. The leader stopped but continued tapping its metal legs on the floor, waiting. The three behind it followed suit. Then the leader crouched and jumped hitting and latching onto the guard's throat. He instinctively threw up both hands to pry the device from his neck, but the legs had penetrated his flesh and he fell to the ground choking until his spirit leaked out and down the metal legs into the glass sphere. The guard lay dead and grey, as the machine moved around the body to face Marcus once more.

Ophilya and Haram were at the door. "Abeline will be mine. I will return, soon." They fled from the room and sped down the corridor. Ophilya stopped at a window overlooking the outer courtyard and waved a signal to a loitering group of men. The men ran to fetch their tethered horses. This was Ophilya's escape plan.

The lead machine continued stalking and crouched

down for a second time before launching itself towards Marcus. Marcus raised his arm quickly in front of his face and the device's legs grabbed hold of his arm.

The soul-machine clenched its legs which started to penetrate through the soft leather sleeves that Marcus wore. Blood started to drip where a needle-sharp leg was entering into Marcus's flesh, and then wisps of his soul sprang forth into the sphere.

Jaryd lurched forward and secured a firm grip on the round cold body. There was no time to carefully ease the legs from their grip, so he pulled hard and threw the machine to the ground. It landed with the glass hemisphere striking the floor, but righted itself onto its legs almost immediately. It moved forward once more, then paused. A small crack had appeared in the glass which lengthened until it spanned the whole circumference. With a loud crack, the glass imploded releasing the spirits held within which faded from existence.

The remaining three devices had circled Jaryd who stood protecting Marcus. Jaryd's sword was in the rack by the door with all of the others. Without that, he had no means of defence against an attack by all of these devices. All three machines creaked and crouched lowering their bodies close to the ground ready to strike.

From the corner of his eye, Jaryd saw a movement in the shadows and a golden glint from a sword. Eva took two strides and launched herself into the fray swinging Jaryd's sword in a complete circle around her head, nearly cutting Jaryd as she landed close to him.

The devices released the tension in their legs as Eva continued her circular swing crouching at ground level. Her stroke made perfect contact with the soul-machines, severing their legs with a single blow. The sword continuing in its circular path, Eva released it from her grip sending it arrow-straight to embed itself within the dark wooden walls.

The disabled devices rocked on their half-legs as Jaryd, Marcus and Eva approached and released the ensnared spirits with a firm crack under the heels of their boots.

Ophilya and Haram had fled the grounds, but they would eventually be hunted down, being pursued by half of the King's guards. In any case, their motives were now quite clear and the damage that Haram had caused his clerik movement would subdue his plans for many years to come.

Start of a New Era

Over the last few months, there was seldom a week or even a day that passed by without some form of celebration. Whether this consisted of a full-blown party complete with minstrels, street entertainment and feasting, or a simple spontaneous out spilling of merriment from an inn, a reason was not needed.

Since the day of Alvar's defeat, the mood in Abeline and surrounding towns and villages was raised. Spring had recently arrived after a short but sharp winter. Even the blossom coating the trees seemed more resplendent.

It was six months since the death of Annea. Although her body had never been recovered for a decent burial, Eva still laid flowers next to a carved headstone alongside so many others which had been set in a quiet part of a small orchard. Stones marking the lives of those that had fallen during battle and in the tyrannical years that had gone before.

Jaryd was sitting alongside Tiana as they played and told stories to a group of young children. Of course, the young boys only wanted to hear about the battles and what it was like travelling through death. Subjects which Jaryd was not happy about recalling, but he did give in to their constant pressure and told partly-true stories of bravery and sorcery. Stories which could've happened, but never actually did, but still were convincing enough to produce the required gasps and exclamations of grossness from his audience.

Tiana and her group of girls were arranging wildflowers and talking of brave knights and damsels in distress, handsome princes and their valiant deeds. They forced her to tell of Marcus's bravery and how he defeated Alvar. The truth was irrelevant and Tiana obliged with the required tales.

A small girl, after quietly concentrating for the duration of the stories and linking small pretty flowers into a chain, stood up and walked to Jaryd. He and his listeners paused and looked up at her.

"This is for Eva. She looks so sad." The girl presented, in both hands, a wonderful creation of chained flowers. "It'll make her a princess," she said with a shy smile.

Whilst it was true that on the inside Eva was still grieving for the loss of her mother and for not even knowing her father, she always carried an outwardly happy expression. It would take a lot of study to see past her charade, or maybe someone that could see inside her. Whatever talents this small girl possessed, she had seen Eva's sorrow.

"Thank you. She'll love this." Jaryd stood and bowed kindly to the little girl, then headed off to where he suspected Eva was once again.

He walked through the arched, hedged wall of the orchard and looked to the far corner. The trees were in full blossom and Eva, wearing a shoulderless white dress, was sitting on her feet alone and talking quietly. A one-way conversation with her parents directed through the gravestone. He crept closer not wanting to disturb her, and sat down close.

"Hi! That's pretty." Eva looked at the chain Jaryd was holding.

"It's a gift," he replied, "from the girls," he added quickly.

"Well, I didn't think you'd made it," Eva joked.

"I can be delicate and gentle too you know."

Eva bent her head forward as Jaryd placed the flower crown on her soft hair.

"The girls were right. You do look like a princess."

She punched him playfully on the arm.

Marcus and Tiana walked into the orchard and met Eva, closely followed by Jaryd, leaving. The new King and his wife were circled by giggling girls singing and chanting a schoolyard rhyme, "Eva and Jaryd sitting under a tree, k-i-s-s-i-n-g." Eva walked silently straight past the couple. Jaryd followed, raised his eyebrows and shrugged his shoulders, then followed in Eva's footsteps back to the castle.

"I told you," said Tiana. "You're so blind." She followed Jaryd quickly trying to catch up, leaving Marcus standing confused.

It was six months since Marcus took the throne, or more precisely, since Jaryd and Eva had despatched Alvar and Varga. But Marcus and his wife were the true heirs, and there were certainly no objections from any quarter.

The new order in Abeline was beginning to be

established, fair taxation, a decent wage, and the establishment of considerably better schooling and education for all. Education was backed and assisted by the cleriks, who were trying to introduce a sense of duty to the citizens. Not a forced subservience but two-way respect for each other and the state.

The vast army that Alvar had created and conscripted was greatly reduced in numbers, much to the relief of many of its members who were only too relieved to return back to their original trades, and to earn a decent living. Gone were the overblown generals who supported and encouraged Alvar during his reign, mostly exiled and banished from Abeline.

The state of the city's finances was in complete disarray. Alvar had spent far too much on supporting his army which he thought would be the key to his continued rule. And he'd recklessly thrown money at various mercenary groups too. Spending on amenities and civic facilities, the core structures of a civilised society, was zero, excluding what was afforded to himself and his luxuries.

With yet another poor harvest the year before, this situation would take some time to recover. But individual outlooks were positive. At last, there was light at the end of the tunnel, and a greater nation beckoned for all those that were willing to supply the required effort.

It was mid-morning as Jaryd entered Abeline's council chambers at the request of Marcus. As he entered the room, he was greeted by a number of familiar faces.

Marcus had seconded part of the Wodel council to assist him, and they stood to greet Jaryd as he entered to take his seat.

Jaryd was a little confused at his summons to this meeting. The operations of most civic functions were already starting to take shape. In fact, most were already running better than the equivalents in Wodel. He sat attentively.

"Jaryd, my friend," Marcus began. "You are right to show confusion on your face."

He immediately attempted to straighten his face but it was always his biggest fault. He showed his feelings on his face like an open book. Perhaps that was why he was so trusted amongst those now present.

"Varga's soul." And bluntness was thankfully one of Marcus's traits.

"I have it safe, still."

"No doubt. And your plans for it?"

Jaryd searched the room and weighed up each character and their allegiance which was engraved upon their spirit. He placed a small bottle on the table, and pushed it to the centre.

Whilst some sat forward in their chairs for a better view, most remained calm and did not move.

"I have no plans for that which I carry. It is true that whilst I carry it, it is safe. But it also pulls to its owner like a fishing line. I fear it may eventually be taken."

"Thank you, my friend, for bearing this burden. I know your mind will be greatly set at ease soon."

"If we open the bottle there is a chance the contents

will find their master." But Jaryd knew what was coming next.

"And if we don't dispose of it?"

"It will be found, eventually." Whether this was in Jaryd's lifetime, his successor's, or from a location where it would be hidden, time was on Varga's side.

"Jaryd, it is your decision."

"I relinquish that duty. Any man here can take this and hide it or open it."

"We have no real choice. It's either now or later." Marcus reached to the centre of the table and took hold of the bottle. He took a last look at Jaryd for approval, unstoppered the bottle, turned to his right and inverted it. There were no signs of disapproval.

All those seated at the table stood and peered at the cracking essence as it sank into the floor. Marcus offered the bottle back to Jaryd.

"Burn it. There will still be traces left."

Marcus walked to the smouldering grate and stoked it to a fierce heat, then placed the bottle and stopper into the whiteness where it began to quickly melt.

The council watched as the bottle's form dissolved in the flames, the last remains of Varga's captured soul evaporating into the air. Marcus returned to his seat and indicated that the meeting should resume.

The atmosphere within the chamber appeared more relaxed, as if a heavy burden had been removed. But it was a burden that Jaryd had bore for the past months, and that burden had now changed to anxiety about the haste in which Varga's soul would pass even beyond his reach.

"Now that just leaves one outstanding issue."

"You mean, what became of Ophilya?" Jaryd finished Marcus's sentence.

"Indeed."

"All I know is all that I have already told. She helped me, but I presume that she will expect me to return the deed. Or perhaps we already have with the death of her husband."

"But will she contact Varga? Is she to continue Alvar's practices?"

"I cannot guess, and would not want to speculate. There are many avenues open to her now. Which one she takes only time will tell."

Of course, that was not the answer the council members wanted to hear, but there was no arguing. Speculation as to her future plans would be pointless.

Under a shady parasol within Alvar's favourite courtyard, Tiana and Eva sat attempting to concentrate on sewing some detail onto baby clothing for Tiana's expected child. The atmosphere hung heavy with questions that Tiana had little confidence in asking, and no right to either.

"Eva?" Tiana began and waited courteously for Eva's attention.

"Yes," she replied slowly and quietly, trying to keep her attention focused and trying to dissuade Tiana from the full flow of the interrogation she expected after the earlier encounter and the child's playground song.

"Jaryd," Tiana said.

"Here we go," Eva thought. It wasn't really anybody's business but her own. Nevertheless, Tiana is a good friend.

"He is looking after you as he promised that he would, isn't he?"

"Ti, yes he is. And don't look at me like that."

But Tiana continued to stare silently at her, expecting and waiting for a fuller explanation.

Eva threw her stitching into her lap and looked Tiana directly in the eyes. "When we, when we visited Varga's lands, our spirits were joined. Only partly, but it lets me see him more clearly now. I can see him, his kindness, his caring, through his eyes. I like what I see Tiana. It makes my tummy fizz."

"And does his tummy 'fizz' when he looks at you?"

"I don't know. I guess so. Some things I don't think need to be said."

"Perhaps it would be wise to ask before you make a fool of yourself," Tiana suggested.

"I'm not a child, Ti." Eva was the only person to call her that. Not even her husband had a pet name for her. Well, not one he used in public.

"I know Eva." Tiana reached over and squeezed Eva's hand. "I know."

Time Passes, End of Heroes

It was early morning and Jaryd stood by two fine horses laden with saddlebags. The last of the late spring frosts had departed, and the thaw meant roads and mountain passes would now be fully open. The sun shone bright and warmed his dark shirt; his cloak was packed amongst the other clothing and supplies on his horse.

Abeline's townsfolk were about their normal business but a small gathering had started to form just outside the now permanently open gates.

Marcus, Tiana and Eva appeared around the corner of the stables and walked briskly toward Jaryd, Eva holding the Queen's hand who was obviously late into her pregnancy.

"Are you all packed?" Marcus enquired.

"Yes, I think so. I think Eva's managed to pack everything." Jaryd pointed to the bulging bags and looked sarcastically at Eva. She returned a friendly sneer.

"I hope you still have some extra room. It looks like there may be more to pack." Tiana pointed at the swelling assembly at the gate.

"I was actually hoping for a quiet departure. None of this undeserved fuss."

"Your friends want to show their gratitude, and it looks like word has got out." Marcus looked toward Tiana who had a wry smile on her face.

Marcus and Jaryd clasped each other's forearms and

pulled themselves into a comradely embrace, slapping each other firmly on the back.

"You are, of course, both very welcome here. Treat Abeline as your home and visit often." As much as Marcus had to remain dignified as King, he could not restrain his emotions and secretly wiped away a tear as he made to brush his hair from his face.

They released each other and Jaryd stood back and turned to Tiana offering her his hand for a courteous farewell. She stepped forward, rejected his hand and put her arms around his neck kissing both cheeks as Eva, with a slight expression of envy on her face, looked on.

"Don't be so formal amongst your friends Jaryd."

"Thank you. For everything. We owe you…"

"Nothing. It is we who owe you everything," Tiana interrupted.

They stood close to each other as Eva said her farewells to Marcus. "Good luck with your baby."

"Thank you. Maybe your children will play with ours in the near future." Tiana glanced at Eva and then back to Jaryd's embarrassed and shocked face. She kissed him once more suppressing his protestations of innocence. Inevitably his fondness for Eva had become too transparent, but surely any such relationship was unlikely.

Jaryd led the horses by the reins as Eva followed at his side, Tiana and Marcus behind them. A hesitant crowd began to cast petals as they neared the gate and a ripple of applause erupted, soon rising to drown out all other sounds. The exit was blocked by the throng and they had to force a path through. As they did, gifts of thanks were bestowed upon them; freshly baked bread, spiced meats and other assortments of food and drink, all welcome for the journey ahead.

The gathering thinned out and they had said their last farewells when a young girl ran from her mother's grip towards Eva. Eva turned and stopped then bent down to talk to the child. She was young and her mother was not much older than Eva herself.

The girl stretched out her hands revealing a beautifully made daisy chain. Made with such care and love as those she'd made in her childhood for Annea. She reached to Eva's wrist and wrapped the chain loosely around it.

"That will keep you safe and happy. It's full of fairy magic," the girl announced.

Eva said nothing but just grabbed the child and hugged her tight. A motherly hug that she hoped to one day give to her own children, but a hug that she could now relate to those received from her mother Annea.

A short distance down the path they mounted their horses and rode slowly on.

"Don't look back," Eva told Jaryd.

"Why? Is that some superstitious nonsense you've learned?"

"No. I just don't want to cry."

Jaryd looked at her with admiration, but whether she looked back or not, he could see that she wept freely.

West, through the barren wasteland and to another town in hardship, or east back through Wodel? When they reached the crossroads out of sight of the people in Abeline, Jaryd made the decision to go north on the barely used path over the river, through the mountains, and into the leafy forests. Whether they'd settle in the next town or village they arrived at, or that they'd continue on an endless journey hadn't been decided. What was decided was that this was their time, a well-earned respite from the spiritual struggles of others, and a time for peace.

In Abeline Marcus was well on the way to recover from the damage caused to the city and its people during the tyrannical rule of Alvar. Together with part of the Wodel council and the clerik order, they would continue to rebuild, be fair, and prosper.

But nobody could ignore the threat still posed by Varga. Whilst it would take time for him to recover from the loss of part of his soul, and he had no apparent desire to rule in the territory of the living, he had a score to settle with Jaryd.

After a full day's ride, Jaryd and Eva had navigated a passage through the cold mountains and had descended the gentle lower slopes to the outer edge of the forest. The trees would provide more warmth for their rest as night was approaching fast.

A few hundred yards deeper into the forest, where the cold mountain slopes disappeared from view, the pair decided to make camp in the next available clearing.

Jaryd's body and senses felt a sudden chill and briefly shuddered. He looked to Eva who rode on unperturbed. This wasn't due to a night breeze from the mountains, it was an unnatural indication of trouble ahead, a sense that he had forgotten for several months.

From the darkness of the dense trees, a group of five mounted men emerged to their front, left and right. The men were lit up by flaming torches held aloft, and it was apparent that these were the mercenaries who attacked when they first made their way to Abeline many months ago.

"Eva, turn. Run!"

They both pulled hard on their reins drawing their horses to a startled halt, and about turned to flee back in the direction of the mountains. But, as they turned, two more from this small army closed in alarming Eva's horse so as to cause it to rear up onto its hind legs. Eva wrestled with the reins and struggled to maintain her seat but the horse kicked, dislodged her and threw her to the ground.

She lay still on the grass for a few seconds as she regained her senses and watched as her horse careered off out of sight. Jaryd had his horse under control and was backing up and away from the closing men.

He heard two twangs and thumps then his horse faltered and went down onto its knees. He could see the ends of crossbow bolts protruding from his mount's neck, deeply embedded in its throat. It fell to its side rolling Jaryd off towards where Eva now stood, kicking its legs in its final stages of life.

Jaryd attempted to reach his sword, but the beast had collapsed upon it. Eva's weapons were on her bolted horse, so the pair stood unarmed, and waited. He felt the cold shiver once more. It did not originate from within this surrounding army.

There was no way to protect Eva from all of the men but he stood between her and the direction where the chill appeared to stem from.

Two of the horses directly in front of the cowering couple parted slightly and a lone rider rode up and dismounted. He removed his cloak's hood from his head and raised his stare from the ground and into Jaryd's eyes, it was Varga.

Varga tilted his head to one side and studied Jaryd and then Eva behind him.

"You took something of mine, and it's now time for it to be returned," Varga spoke steadily and patiently.

He's weak and his soul is incomplete, Jaryd thought. He hasn't realised that I've let his sought-after part free, but did not admit this.

"That which I took from you, it stinks. But what will you give me for its return?" Jaryd's words made no impression.

"You know that I'll take it from your dead body whether you agree to hand it over or not." Jaryd knew that his fate was in Varga's hands, but importantly he also knew that Varga never regained his lost part. "Kill him!"

"No, wait!" Jaryd pleaded. "It's gone," he blurted out. But both now knew that Varga was weakened and desperate to regain his whole soul.

There was a pause and it was clear that Varga was visibly infuriated at this news.

"You took something of mine, and now it's gone forever," Varga shouted, and studied Jaryd's face and how he looked at Eva. "So now I must take something of yours." He nodded at the bowmen who had shot his horse, and a single bolt flew past Jaryd and sank into Eva's chest. A second later another shot struck her and she fell to the ground.

"No!" Jaryd bellowed an inhuman roar which flooded the ears of all around him, startling both horses and riders.

He collapsed in grief to his knees where Eva lay bleeding, composed himself for a moment taking a deep breath, opened his mind with all the experience he had, filling the hearts and minds of all the surrounding men with his presence, and wrenched their souls clean from their human bodies sending them beyond Varga's dominion and instantly destroying them. Varga's army collapsed lifelessly to the ground as the last remnants of their departing shattered essence dissolved into the earth.

Varga picked himself from the leafy ground and observed the state of his body. It was far from complete, parts of his form were missing. His essence was dripping into the ground as his shape began to disintegrate. He fell on all fours and lifted his head to curse Jaryd, but the words never formed through his fragmenting mouth. His arms and legs sank into the earth followed by his head like a man submerging in quicksand. Only a few wisps of his spirit remained darting over the surface, then they were gone.

Jaryd lifted Eva's body into his lap and with a shaky hand moved her hair from her face.

"Eva, there's so much I wanted to tell you, to show you." Jaryd tried to speak through uncontrolled tears.

"Jaryd," Eva spoke softly with fading breaths.

"Don't talk Eva." He wanted to tell her to rest, but they both knew her body could not be healed this time.

"It's not cold. It feels warm and bright, beautiful." Eva, though drifting away, had a content expression on her face.

She reached up with her hand and wrapped it around his neck, pulled herself up, and kissed him slowly on his mouth.

Jaryd held her body tightly, stroking her cheeks and hair then felt her human form lose its spirit and become cold.

"Be at peace, my friend, my angel, my love."

The sweetness of her face pulled at his heart. His tears flowed without restraint dripping onto her.

"Why didn't we have more time?" From a distance, his roar of anger echoed through the forest and off the mountains. Then all was quiet.

Eva passed into death. She waited in the gloomy realms and watched. It was strangely quiet, and she half expected to see the souls of the recently killed mercenaries slowly drift further into the darkness. But they had been destroyed by Jaryd.

Her attachment to the living world was strong and bound with love for Jaryd who sat and wept alone. But this bond was not enough to delay her passing to where Varga ruled. She didn't feel despair or cold, but a strange warmth within her made her tingle, from her toes through her body and down her arms. She was grieving for the ones she had left behind, but was not crying inside.

Close to where she stood, Varga's essence formed a shady dark figure. It was incomplete. Something was missing. Part of his spirit's core was absent, disposed of by Jaryd after Alvar was defeated, but never recaptured by Varga.

His form was visible enough to show his wide grin and his coldness became stronger as he silently approached Eva. Eva did not move. She was curious.

"There is no escape now. Only one way to go from here."

Surprisingly, Eva had no fear of this creature, but no pity either. She despised what he had done and what he did to others.

She felt a burning sensation in her stomach, replacing the butterflies and tingling of earlier. This couldn't be how it felt to be dead, to be under the control of Varga, lord of souls; it felt too delightful. She remembered her father, and recalled times they shared together. And her mind was also filled with events that she did not share with him in the living world, yet these visions were so vivid. It was as if his memories were pouring into her own mind.

Eva watched Varga as he stood within arm's reach and slowly raised a skinny, cloaked arm. He leaned forward to grab her, to take her, but as she watched curiously at his narrow fingers she felt no terror.

Varga forced his body forward but his hand could not touch Eva. He studied his hand and fingers, they had simply ceased to exist where he had tried to contact the girl in front of him. He raised his look to Eva's face and opened his eyes wide with shock. Eva's face and body were glowing warm and bright. Short pointed beams of light wandered from her projecting chest pulling at her, forcing her to travel beyond Varga's domain. He now knew the recipient of Godwyn's gift. Godwyn's message of hope and love had been kept secret within his daughter since his death, and now it was being awakened and assimilated.

Varga blocked her way, and stood between her and the closed gates of heaven, desperate to prevent Eva from fulfilling Godwyn's hopes that the gates should be reopened. But his powerless essence could not restrain her now. Without hesitation and full of eagerness, Eva flew from this place, passing total destruction on what remained of Varga as her spirit forged a path through him and his world.

The bindings that Varga had put on the gates into the light were gone. The barred entrance faded open and Eva was at rest and with her father. A gleaming path cut through the dark swamps of death and led to these open gates for all that were worthy to follow. There she waited.

Time Passes, End of Heroes

The next morning, two guards from a travelling party of cleriks rode into the circle of the dead mercenaries, guided there by stories of strange cries in the night. They dismounted cautiously with swords drawn, and slowly investigated the bodies forming the circle.

Their masters arrived shortly afterwards and began examining the mercenaries too, but withdrew confused as there were no visible wounds that could possibly have caused their demise.

One clerik was sitting by Eva, the cause of her death obvious. But the man, Jaryd, holding her, his death could not be explained. The tracks of his tears had dried and his eyes were closed, but his face depicted a man who'd found eternal happiness.

Together their bodies sat, but in heaven their spirits flew.

The gates are open.

Soul Thieves

Tempus fugit
Carpe diem